PANDORA

BOOKS ALSO BY DAWN BATES

Becoming Annie – The Biography of a Curious Woman (2020)

The Trilogy of Life Itself:

Friday Bridge – Becoming a Muslim, Becoming Everyone's Business (2nd Edition, 2017)

Walaahi – A firsthand account of living through the Egyptian Uprising and why I walked away from Islaam (2017)

Crossing The Line – A Journey of Purpose and Self-Belief (2017)

The Sacral Series:

Moana – One Woman's Journey Back to Self (2020)

Leila – A Life Renewed One Canvas at a Time (2020)

ALSO PUBLISHED BY DAWN PUBLISHING

Becoming the Champion – V1 Awareness by Korey Carpenter (2020)

Unlocked – Discover Your Hidden Keys by Carmelle Crinnion (2020)

Break Down to Wake Up – Journey Beyond the Now by Jocelyn Bellows (2020)

Slave Boy – Book 1 Democ'Chu Series by Nath Brye (2020)

Standing in Strength – Inspirational Stories of Power Unleashed by Laarni Mulvey (2021)

PANDORA

MELTING THE ICE – ONE DIVE AT A TIME

DAWN BATES

DAWN PUBLISHING

Published by Dawn Publishing
www.dawnbates.com
The moral right of the author has been asserted.

For quantity sales or media enquiries, please contact the publisher at the website address above.

Cataloguing-in-Publication entry is available from the British Library.

ISBN: 978-1-913973-20-9 (paperback)
978-1-913973-21-6 (ebook)

Book cover design – Jerry Lampson
Publishing Consultant – Linda Diggle

Disclaimer: The material in this publication is of the nature of general comment only and does not represent professional advice. It is not intended to provide specific guidance for particular circumstances and should not be relied on as the basis for any decision to take action or not to take action on any matters which it covers.

CONTENTS

PREFACE

I first heard about freediving back in the late 1990s and thought it would be a pretty cool thing to try, but living in the UK at the time, there was no way you would find me in the cold North Sea water. Newquay on the West Coast wasn't much better, and other than the masses of surfers the town has to offer, there are just far too many people there for my liking.

Scuba diving with tanks were the way forward for me, but freediving always fascinated me. I would practice holding my breath for as many lengths as I could as I trained for my 2-mile open water swims. 25 metres, 50 metres… 'bubble bubble breath' turned into 'bubble, bubble, stillness, bubble bubble breath, stillness' and repeat over and over again. It was always a challenge for me to see how far I could swim under water without coming up for air, and I found I much preferred swimming under water than I did above the water; hence the nicknames Mermaid and Dolphin I was given years earlier when at school.

Freediving isn't a new thing, in fact it is something that has been used around the world in places such as the Pacific Islands, the Mediterranean, the Indian Ocean Islands such as Mauritius and Madagascar, The Caribbean and Cabo Verde for over 8000 years by traditional fisherman using spears made of sharpened sticks.

Being agile, fast and responsive to be able to catch the fish for food meant freediving was the better option, and those who simply stood in the water were often left standing empty handed, and the family and community would go hungry. Freediving was not the competitive sport it is today; it was a necessity.

Pearl hunters and sponge divers would make their money and find their place of favour in royal palaces dating back as far Ancient Greece. If you have read any Homer, or the words of Plato, seen the stories of Cleopatra, you will know all about sponge baths, and it was the sponge divers of the times who were some of the earliest freedivers.

Over the last 500 years, freedivers have been used to destroy underwater barricades so ships can pass. Many messages and supplies were passed secretly from submarine to ship, and allies in enemy lands used to salvage any useful equipment from previously sunken ships. Used to scout enemy lines, check the seabed's looking for anything that could cause damage to the hull or propellers of the vessel, freedivers were often overlooked and under paid for their services to the military. They were also some of the fittest and calmest members of all the military squadrons due to the breathing and mental alertness that came with being a freediver.

If you have been snorkelling or diving you'll know that it is very easy to lose your way, along with losing hours of time underneath the surface mesmerised by the abundance of corals, marine life and the curiosity of what is past that next rock. Holding your breath and descending 20 metres under the water's surface is not something to take lightly and although freediving doesn't have the same impact the scuba gear has on you, it can still be incredibly dangerous, and it is always recommended you go with someone. Diving to deeper depths with your scuba gear on your back may give you longer under the water, and you may be able to go to deeper depths, but the dangers of running out of air, or the noise and bubbles disturbing marine life which does not wish to be disturbed can also be dangerous.

The ocean may be a beautiful place, it may hold more life than we can even begin to contemplate, but it is also a powerful force of energy, underestimated by so many. The ocean isn't a place for ego, nor is it simply a place to lose yourself in the moment. Risks of asphyxia, latent hypoxia are commonplace for many freedivers, wanting to go that little bit deeper, for that little bit longer. The first 10 metres the human body goes under water, it is subjected to twice as much pressure as on the surface, which means the pressure on the organs intensifies. The deeper we go under the water, the next level of atmospheric pressure we encounter and the physiology of our body changes and starts becoming manipulated, with spaces in the body which contain air being compressed and the gases within our bodies start making changes to the way our blood and nervous systems operate.

The photos may look cool, but the damage to mind

and body are not so cool. What starts out as a 'letting go' of the pressures of the mind, of 'becoming one' with ourselves, soon becomes a bit of an 'addiction to the freefall', the part of the dive which is described as 'the most beautiful part of the dive' and normally happens around 13 metres down, and the point at which the buoyancy pushes you back to the surface stops and you start falling to the bottom of the ocean. Sounds scary, but for the freedivers this stage is where the narcotic effect kicks in due to the nitrogen dissolving in the blood stream.

It is estimated that there is somewhere in the region of 6000 known freedivers in the world, not including all those scattered around the islands mentioned above, and the Sama people from the islands of the Philippines. As a people who have been spearfishing, and thus freediving for hundreds of years, their bodies have adapted and their spleens have become 50% larger than the average person, which means they can process oxygen more efficiently and stay underwater longer.

With this knowledge becoming more and more widespread, the competition is on for the 'professional' freedivers to go even deeper than before, and for longer, leading to an average of 100 dying every year. The Sama people can do it through generations of evolution, and many competitive divers are simply trying to do it through mind over matter, dying either during the dive or after they have returned to the surface. The pressure on the organs during a freedive causes a weakening of them, and over time the organs start to fail. Some die hours or days after the dive, whilst some die immediately after the dive. Others just can't get that 'high' anymore so push themselves further and as they realise they need to return to the surface it is too late. Even considering these figures, and the damage it can do to the body, freediving is still one of the fastest growing sports around the world.

Other sports such as synchronised swimming used aspects of freediving breath techniques, and there is now a whole range of competitive sports and activities such as underwater photography, hockey, rugby, football and target shooting, all pushing people and their bodies to the underwater limits.

The competitive life of Instagram is also adding its own kind of pressure as inexperienced divers and photographers push themselves further underwater to get that all important selfie just for the likes, followers and notoriety.

Today's modern sport of freediving is a long way from the days of spearfishing, pearl hunting, sponge diving, reclaiming sunken treasures and passing secrets from ships and military vessels. Not many people know of the fascinating history of this sport, nor do they understand the impact it has on their bodies.

The freedivers used in warfare and many undercover ops such as the naval seals are now being glamourised in movies with A-list celebrities. Back in 1964, Ian Fleming's James Bond movie *You Only Live Twice* featured Kissy Suzuki, a Japanese Ama diver, a livelihood which dates back to over 2000 women, and links many of the mermaid tales to the long-haired beauty sitting on a rock with pearls in her hair.

Freediving is the stuff of legend, and the science world is fascinated by the 6000 freedivers around the world and how they betray all scientific data going to the extreme depths that they do. Many countries such as Sweden, The Bahamas and Alaska are home to some of the world's best freediving spots, and all for very different reasons.

Hundreds of freediving competitions are held all over the world each year; with women taking up most of the places and performing better than the men. With many blackouts happening either on the surface or the rise to the surface, safety is paramount in all competitions; but people still die and more people are taking up the sport. For some it is simply the next level of diving, for others it is wanting to push themselves to the next level of mind over matter, and for others it is the pure adrenalin rush and vanity aspects. The latter ones are those most likely to die or change their perspective on the sport very quickly.

For people like Pandora, it was simply the next step in the healing journey of numbing the pain in the ice-cold waters and silencing the voices in her head. She, and people like her are the ones who discovered the beauty in the pain, transcending beyond what they ever thought possible for themselves, whilst discovering a world more beautiful beneath the surface than the one they experienced above.

With love,

Dawn

To find out more, please visit my website www.dawnbates.com where you can listen to the podcasts which accompany this book and the entire Sacral Series collection of conversations and books.

ONE
ATLANTIC LAKE

The sun was scorching hot, and we had been in the doldrums for a few days. The ocean was so calm, like a lake, a deep blue inviting me in, calling my name, calling me away from all the people who had surrounded me for the last few weeks.

I wanted the serenity of the water. The silence it offered, and the feeling of being at home in the water. Leaping off the ship into the Atlantic Ocean I was filled with so much joy. Here I was in the middle of the Atlantic, in the Southern Hemisphere, about to go for a swim.

The water was warm on the surface, and crystal clear. I wanted the silence, I wanted to go beneath the surface and swim as far away from that ship as I possibly could. I could have swum across the surface but when you have the soul of a mermaid, and a curious mind like mine, there is only one direction to go in, and that is down.

With my goggles on I dived down, and down, and the further down I went the cooler the water became. The silence was just what I wanted, and with the sun shining through the water, the rays of light cutting through like crystal, I felt the joy rising within me. A deep, vibrant blue like no blue I had ever seen before. Not royal blue, not navy blue, not even a sky blue on a summer's day, just a beautifully stunning ocean blue of my very own.

The deeper I went, the colder the water, and it felt great. After having been so humidly hot onboard deck for the last four weeks, it was so good to be naturally cold, and the silence of the underwater world soothed my mind and soul as much as the water nourished my body.

I was home, and I didn't want to return to the surface, but knew I had to. I had to return to the ship, I had to get to land so I could call my boys and let them know I had just been swimming in the middle of the Atlantic. I had to let them know that this journey of self-discovery, the time away from them researching content for my new books, and promoting my existing ones, was filled with moments I wanted to share with them, memories we would recreate together once I had my own boat. I knew they would be proud of me. I just knew it.

And so back to the surface I returned, with the sight of dozens of legs wiggling in the water from those also sailing on the ship, I knew I hadn't drifted too far away. The water was getting warmer, and then I heard their voices. For a split second I wanted to return to the depths below, but I was a mama, I had a responsibility to my boys, and so I returned back to the others, back on board the ship, back to my bunk where I closed the curtains and lay there until I was required back on deck for night watch.

Lying there I allowed tears of happiness to fall. The immense feeling of joy to wash over me, the gratitude I felt flooded my body, every cell of my being and then I giggled, and wiggled an excited dance in my bunk. I had just been swimming in the middle of the Atlantic Ocean, diving deeper than I had probably gone before unsupervised and witnessed a natural light show of the sun and sea dancing together in perfect harmony. How blessed was I?

With eyes wide open with excitement and then closed to recapture the moments underwater, her face came back to me. Her words of the magical underwater world which opened up to you if you approached her with respect, came back to me like a whispering song. "You'd love it down there".

And she was right, I do love it down there.

TWO

CANDLE BURNS

Staring at the flame, watching it dance, she wondered how long she would be able to hold her hand over it before it burnt, and what that would feel like. It couldn't be worse than the pain she had felt before, this all-encompassing feeling of being swallowed whole by a huge kind of ectoplasm, distorting sound, vision and holding her firmly in its grasp. It hadn't mattered how she'd tried to move to escape it, or even if she'd stayed still, the feelings were the same: trapped, suffocating and being moved along by external forces which took away her own control.

She moved her hand over the flame, feeling the warmth before moving her hand to dip her finger in the melted wax, because that was the fun part, even when she didn't want to hurt herself. She smiled. She had come a long way since the days where she would intentionally burn herself, either by holding her hand over the flame or pouring the wax over her naked skin. She moved her left thumb over the middle of her right palm, feeling the scars on her hand, before moving her hand up her arm where the scars had been left by the hot wax.

She remembered swallowing the screams, closing her mouth so tightly her lips disappeared under her teeth as she pulled them in to hold her breath, whilst she allowed her eyes to roll back into her head at the same time. That part of her life seemed so long ago, and there was no heart-breaking sensations fizzing inside her body anymore. The sadness and fear didn't wash over her anymore. Was she still numb or had she truly healed? What was the difference anyway? Did anyone ever really know, even though there were so many experts out there in the world who spoke of healing, and then in the same breath said we are all whole and complete just the way we are anyway. Did they mean the abusers and the evil who walked the earth are also whole and complete, perfect as they are? Questions she had long since pondered over and had now learnt not to dwell on them.

She picked up her coffee mug, took the last mouthful, and looked out the window. The sun was coming up and it was time to hit the beach. She blew out the candle, walked to the door, grabbed her dive bag and looked back. She loved her cosy home, it was just enough for her, by herself, in this little area of the world. It wasn't for everyone, but for her it was her sanctuary, a home, a place she felt safe in; away from everyone else, and she liked it that way.

It didn't matter how many times she had heard the click of her weight belt; it sent a surge of excitement through her body from the sacred spot in her vagina to the top of her head and to the tips of her toes. It had been a long time since she had allowed any feeling in her body, especially down there. She had blocked it for so long she didn't know if it would ever be able to give her pleasure again. No man had been invited there. No woman either. It was hers, and hers alone; and that was the way it would stay.

The water was cold this morning, and the blue was that dawn dark blue, just the way she liked it. She would get to see it change colour whilst she was down below, returning to the surface each time to a different ocean, different sky and a different temperature. She looked around, there was no one out yet, not a surfer of any kind in sight. She had the water to herself, and no 'Bro' to eye her up or get annoyed at her because she appeared out of nowhere from under the waves. She often surprised many of them as she resurfaced, having been out of sight and below the water for more than fifteen minutes. The looks she'd seen on some of their faces as she removed her mask was one of both surprise and fear, and the same question, "Where the hell did you come from?" written all over their faces. A question she had often wanted to answer with the details of hell she had come from, but she couldn't, it wouldn't be right. For them, for her mum, for the family, for the community she came from, and so she had 'moved through it', 'alchemised it', 'let it go' as so many in the world of spiritual healing had called it. On the street, in the 'real world' they would simply refer to it as 'sucking it up', 'getting on with it' with the enlightened ones on the planet calling it 'transcendence'.

It didn't matter what it was called though, it wouldn't

be right to share the hell with some random sat on their board waiting for the morning waves to take them away into their own world of tubes and ocean magic. It was an unwritten rule of the ocean, you breathe through it, you hand it over to the water and allow whatever it is to be washed away. "A baptism from Poseidon, in Neptune's Church" as others liked to call it.

For her though, it was just the quiet, the beauty and a sense of oneness she had discovered whilst trying to end it all. A happy accident, a surprise awakening, and the gift of life more profound than any baby could ever give a parent; not that she could possibly know that for real, she had never had a baby, but for those she knew who had children, they were nowhere near as at peace as she was, by their own admission. Maybe she knew the wrong people, maybe not, but nothing she heard or read was ever going to convince her that having children was a good idea. They were just playthings for the evil monsters of the world and a chance for people to make up for their own failings in life, to have someone to love them as much as they needed to love someone else. There were too many people in the world anyway, and with the way the world was heading, she didn't think it was wise to bring more people into it to suffer.

All these thoughts were no longer spoken of, well not as much as they used to be. She used to speak them to anyone who was within earshot, a point to prove, a need to be heard, but she realised it was pointless, and the more she spoke, the more her mother suffered. Seeing the wincing pain in her mother's very being on 'that day' had awoken a knowing in her that she had never seen before. So well hidden behind the quiet eyes and polite shyness, a demure nature of subservience, which had fallen to the floor with a crashing sound in Pan's ears, that during a bad night it would still wake her up in cold sweats and an apnea that could end her life in the depths of the ocean. Seeing the flinch in her mother, the one she herself experienced every time he approached her, touched her and said her name, was the same flinch she saw in so many others in his space, and that's when she knew how far the evil travelled; evil bastard that he was, and yet he was loved, adored and worshipped by the masses. Young boys wanted to become him, women wanted to marry him, and girls wanted him to be their daddy.

If only they knew.

THREE
ICE COLD

The sun was shining, the ocean looked inviting, and he was sleeping. It was the year 2000 and the world had not ended on the turn of the millennium. New Year's Eve had been a messy night, especially at midnight as everyone was peaking on the drugs they had taken twenty to thirty minutes before. Everyone was cheering, jumping up and down, hugging each other, kissing their partner and anyone else who happened to be near-by, and he was nowhere to be seen.

"Welcome to the new century," I wished myself, and then carried on dancing. It was yet another anti-climactic New Year's Eve and we had only been married a year. I excused him not being there because it was a 10,000-strong crowd and getting anywhere always took the pair of us ages. We knew too many people, too many people knew us, or at least thought they knew us. How could anyone know anyone, when none of us really knew ourselves? I knew I didn't know myself but being determined to 'get it right' whatever 'it' was, I always came across as if I knew what I was doing, like I was the confident one. What a lie I was living. I didn't know what confidence was and wouldn't know if it came up and bit me on the arse. I had moments of confidence and could step into the woman I needed to be when walking onto a stage or picking up the phone and asking for the sale, but as a woman, as me? Confidence eluded me at every turn; except when I stepped on the dancefloor or into the water.

I didn't want to wake him, so I left a note, telling him I had gone to the beach. Stepping out into the street of a country I didn't know, which had a language I wasn't expecting to find, felt really exciting. I had foolishly presumed they would speak English, but hearing the locals speak, I felt both foolish and ignorant, but I was also now having a mini adventure all by myself. I felt so free, like I was in my own world, making up the rules of my life as I went along. I smiled as I passed people in the street. They smiled back, and by the time I got to the beach I had already figured out how to say good morning to the locals 'Haloogikpin' – or rather, I thought that was they were saying for 'good morning'. It could have been anything, but it was said with a smile so who was I to doubt their friendliness? It was still early and there were only locals around, all the tourists were probably still in bed nursing hangovers or catching up on sleep from working their arses off before they had arrived.

I was surprised to not see any surfers in the water, and so very few dog walkers, but the local culture and economy didn't really lend itself to 'Peaches the Poodle' being walked along the beach at first light, more like opening the door and letting the mutt take itself for a walk. Taking my shib shib off and rolling up the legs of my jeans, I stepped into the water. "Ooo bugger that's cold!" I laughed stepping back out of the water but staying close enough that the waves would still come up to my feet. I remember thinking I could 'ease my way in' but this water was far too cold, no wonder all the hotels had large pools! I wondered what it would be like to live here, having a dog to walk along the beach every day, and being too chicken to go into the ice-cold water. How could it be cold? It was summer! Maybe it was too early in the day, but I couldn't see how this water could ever get to a temperature I would be happy swimming in. I kept walking, the water teasing my feet, numbing them and freezing them with each wave. I couldn't do it, it was too cold, so no ocean swimming for me this week then. Great! A week of longing to be in the water but not being brave enough to freeze my face off just for the pleasure of playing in the ocean.

"Too cold for you?" I turned around in the direction of the words to see a woman walking out of the ocean carrying a snorkel and mask, wearing just bikini bottoms and a long-sleeved wet suit top.

"You seriously have not just been snorkelling in there have you?" I asked. "Bloody hell! I'm impressed!"

We both laughed and smiled at each other. "I was going to go for a paddle, but I think my insides disappeared into one another at the temperature of the first wave touching my toes."

"Not used to cold water then?" she asked.

"Only for drinking, or swimming in, but this isn't cold, this is bloody freezing!" I replied, still shivering at the thought of the water.

"Well you are in Alaska, there are no Caribbean temperatures here you know," she teased.

"You're not kidding! And I feel a bit embarrassed to be honest with you, I thought everyone here spoke English, but people have been saying 'haloogikpin' to me this morning."

Her laugh was a bit unexpected and I started to feel really stupid. "They've been saying 'haloogikpin' to you have they?" She smiled. "They must like you then, feel you are one of us already, except for the fact you are wearing flip flops," she said pointing to my shib shib. "Haloogikpin is mainly spoken in Northern Alaska, and I am guessing it was the older ones you saw on your walk to the beach this morning who spoke with you then?"

"Yes, they looked like Eskimos, sorry Innuits! Oh my days, I don't even know what the correct term is to use! So did I say it correctly?" I said flustering.

"You said it pretty well actually, better than most of us who don't speak Inupiaq, that's the name of the language you heard this morning by the way. I can see why they said it to you as well, you have that friendly, old energy about you they would have spotted a mile away. Most of us here in Alaska speak English, with Spanish being the next spoken language…"

"Spanish? Really? I would have thought Russian, or is that a big 'no no' considering the history of Alaska?" I asked.

"Well, you're not a typical visitor to these parts are

you? Most come for the surfing, diving, climbing or fishing. They don't care for the history or the etiquette, they just want the adventure or the money from the ocean. Either that, or they are big oil and gas companies who don't give a fuck about anyone or anything else but raping everything and everyone they can get their hands on." The words came out of her mouth with a mix of passion, hate and surprise mixed together with a welcoming dismissal of those who were apparently 'raping' the area.

Changing the subject I asked, "Aren't you cold? I hope I am not keeping you from something?"

"Getting a bit nippy, and I am on my way to get breakfast. Come join me if you want?" she offered.

"Okay, thank you. I was going to go and get coffee after my walk along the beach anyway, and well…." I said turning around to see how far we had walked… "I guess we have walked a fair bit and it would be nice to have a coffee with you. Thank you." And as if by magic, her clothes appeared in a pile on the floor in front of us.

"I like to walk back to my clothes, helps the oxygen and blood move around my body after a dive and lets the water run off my body," she said, obviously reading my mind.

"Diving? You mean you have been diving in there?"

"Haha, yeah, diving. It's beautiful, and silent under the water. My happy place."

"I know what you mean, well about the ocean being your happy place. I have only dived a couple of times with tanks in a pool, but love swimming underwater and seeing how far I can go down and for how long I can hold my breath."

"So you freedive?"

"Freedive? What's that?"

"The best possible kind of diving. Come on, let's go get that coffee before all the tourists come out to play. No offence."

"None taken. I am not a tourist; I am a local everywhere I go," I smiled.

"If the locals have said haloogikpin to you, you're a local," she answered.

"So are all the locals this friendly?"

"Not really. Mainly suspicious because of the oil and gas companies, but that said, yes we are friendly – it's a loaded question to be honest. We rely on the tourists a lot, we have to, one in eight of us are working in tourism; but we mainly get the ignorant cruisers who come in and pollute the place with their rubbish, even though they have come here to view a beautiful natural landscape. Doesn't make sense to most of us, I mean why come here to this beautiful place and leave your rubbish behind. Plus the cruise liners are second biggest polluters of the water around here next to the big G&O companies, and the fisherman the third biggest polluters."

"Oi, Pan. Stop sharing your dirty laundry in here please. You don't want to scare off the tourists," said a friendly looking man in what looked like his fifties, who also had 'the eyebrow' look, the one which tells you to watch what you are saying, not because of shame or embarrassment but out of protection. He placed two coffees on the table, and a plate of waffles, eggs, sausages and berries before turning and saying, "Should do you ladies nicely, just let me know when you want topping up. And good to see you talking with someone."

"Thanks Noah," she said before cutting the sausages in half and breaking the yolk of the egg, allowing it to ooze over the top of the waffles. "Reindeer sausage, fresh from out back, probably killed at the weekend. And fresh eggs from out in the back garden. Noah makes the best waffles, his wife's recipe, and these berries are from the roads 'over yonder' as Noah likes to say."

"Glad to hear it, I only eat local meat, or happy animals as some of my friends like to say. So your name is 'Pan'. I am guessing that is short for something?"

"Pandora," she answered before putting a mouthful of waffle, eggs and berries into her mouth, then put down her cutlery, closed her eyes and sat back to enjoy the taste sensation.

"I am also guessing they don't see you talk to people very often?" The words were out of my mouth before I could stop them. Story of my life.

"I don't like people, I don't trust people, and I like my own company," she replied after a moment, eyes still closed, still sitting back on the sofa of the booth. "You're different. I don't know why. You just are. I think it was the way you were playful and surprised by how cold the water was, and the way you laughed at yourself. It was endearing."

"Thank you. So I am guessing this is why the ocean is your happy place. You know where you stand with the ocean; she's something you can respect, something that feels like home should, safe, and like she's holding you. She gives you the peace you can't find with others, and you know if things go wrong, it is your responsibility. Not hers…" I hadn't realised it but I was now looking out of the window as if I was speaking directly to the ocean, and Pan was looking at me with a deep interest.

"So you know then. You're one of us," said Pan looking at me, deep within me; and I knew in that moment we both shared a secret of a similar kind. I had no idea if they were the underwater kind, past life kind or of another kind. Only time would tell, but I felt at ease with this woman. There was no pretence about her, she was real, with a rawness about her that I liked. I looked at my watch and knew he would still be sleeping.

"You need to get somewhere?" Pan asked me, noticing I had looked at my watch. "I can help you out whilst you're here if you like. And no, I'm not a tourist guide looking for a new client to impress 'with our rugged, yet beautiful skylines and mountain trails'. I like you, and I don't like anyone. People are mainly arseholes if you ask me, stupid and blind to what is going on right in front of their faces."

"You sound angry, and I didn't think you were trying to impress me. You feel too real for that; and thank you for the compliment. I guess I am a bit like you, from what I can tell. I mean we are only a giggle on the beach, a couple of cups of coffee and a bloody tasty waffle and sausage in, but I tend to think when you know, you know. Instinct and all that." I laughed.

Pan looked at me, again with those piercing, defiant eyes, and her pursed lips. It was weird it looked like she'd had surgery to enhance them, but she didn't seem the sort of person to have vanity surgery; and you know, who am I to ask a perfect stranger about their personal surgery just an hour into knowing them.

"They are good sausages aren't they, and the best bit,"

she said switching into the most professional tour guide voice she could probably muster, "The meat from our lands is not only so delicious, but due to our rugged landscapes, pure air and atmosphere, it is also lean and very healthy for you too. We also like to kill the kosher way, so great for all those concerned about the animals welfare." She smirked at herself, and then winked at me before we both giggled at the perfect intonations in her voice and the way she nailed the empty and vacuous mentality of a tour guide who had repeated the words one hundred times a week and had become bored with their own voice.

"So where do you live? You don't sound like the rest of them. Your accent is different."

"I live up in a place called Bethel. It's not glamourous, but it is quiet; and incredibly beautiful. It's about 400k west of here, across land, and much further by sea. I prefer going by boat, takes much longer and the solitude is perfect. The views are amazing, and I get to see a few people I have met over the years. Sorry, bit of an overshare there," apologised Pan.

"Don't worry about it, I was going to ask you all the questions to your answers anyway. See if it was worth visiting whilst I am here, well, whilst we are here. My husband is back at the hotel sleeping. He'll probably be awake in about an hour."

"Unless you like dogs and small towns, I wouldn't bother if I was you," answered Pan.

"Dogs? I love dogs! Please don't tell me that is the place I can go mushing with the huskies!" I said excitedly.

"Well, you could, but I wouldn't advise it. That's the problem with tourists, and I know you said you are not a 'tourist' as such," she said putting tourist in visual speech marks, "but to go mushing you need to connect with the dogs, they need to trust you, so you will be sat there with one of the men doing all the work, and they're pretty sexist up that way. One look at you and they will be breaking their marriage vows, if they are still married, and attempting to get in your knickers."

"They sound a nice bunch," I said with sarcasm in my voice. "Why do you live there then, if it is so desolate and full of immoral men?"

"I didn't say they were immoral, but I can see why you would jump to that given what I had said. You're fresh meat, and you know – not hitting on you or anything, but – you're a good looking woman, who has a very different look to the women here, and add into that, those who want to get out, start a new life, well they would be the first to buy you a drink; well if alcohol was allowed in Bethel."

"Alcohol is not allowed. Why?" I asked intrigued, thinking it was something to do with Native Indian traditions.

"Because they are drunks, that's why. And the crime levels when they get drunk get really high. Like *really* high. About a quarter of us, according to the wonderful American Census Statistics are 'victims of crime', and although I guess that would be true, that is mainly Joe, Hunter and Seth beating the crap out of eachother over a game of pool, or because one of their dogs got frisky with anothers bitch and got her pregnant."

"You don't like the statistics much, do you?"

"Not really, they don't present the real stories, and some of them are hilarious. We read the papers for comedy if truth be told. The thing to know about us lot up in Bethel, is that we may have a few drunks, we may have a few fights, but we are a tight community, and we have each other's backs. We look out for each other; and we look out for each other's dogs. These big city types that come into Anchorage for the G&O, gas and oil, from 'the big cities' look down on us, and think they know what is going on, but they don't have a fucking clue. They wouldn't know what it takes to live out here and the depths we go to for each other." There was that anger again, and it was directed at the American's outside of Alaska. There was a betrayal behind the words, and then it was gone as quickly as it came. "Another reason I live there is the cold, another is the vistas, the skies and the K300 Dog Sled Races. The community is made up of those families who have lived there for generations, the ones who we look to, those of us who are smart anyway. The rest of us, well, you could say we are either looking for a new life, to find solace or just be in peace."

"Don't those last three all stem from the same place?" I asked.

"Do you always ask questions as deep as this when meeting someone?" smiled Pan. "I like it. Real interest, none of that shallow surface crap."

We continued talking for what seemed like ages, and then I felt a hand on my shoulder and heard the words, "There you are. I thought I might find you in a place like this. Hi, how are you?" said my husband reaching out his hand. "She sorted out the entire itinerary for the week ahead with you then. Or asked the whole history of Alaska in 30 minutes flat?" He kissed me on the top of my head, and sat next to me on the sofa couch, ordered a juice and loads of waffles with maple syrup.

"Not quite the whole history, but most definitely asked some very cool questions. I am not a tour guide by the way. We met on the beach as I came out of the water," replied Pan. "I have offered to show you both some of the sights though because I do like your wife's company. If you are agreeable and want to see the real Anchorage?"

"Yeah, cool. Prefer to meet the locals and eat with you."

"He says eating the 'all Canadian' breakfast," laughed Pan.

"Ha ha, touché! What else should I be eating then… this is just a warmup," laughed my hubby.

"Eat the sausage babe, you'll love it, and the eggs were done perfectly. And have the waffles without the syrup, just the juices and yolk from the sausage and egg. 'Tis gorgeous, I tell thee!" I told him.

More coffee was drunk, stories of our lives were shared, and before we knew it, it was nearly lunchtime. "Well, I have to be going. I have to go and do some training. Come with me if you like? It's not for the feint hearted though. You will get to see the landscape with a local… and you will need something more than those flip flops," Pan laughed at me.

"You came out in your shib shib? Ha ha, you and your bloody shib shib!"

"I am guessing shib shib is the Arabic for flip flop?" questioned Pan.

"Yeah, and she lives in them, then moans her feet are

cold and needs to put on her fluffy socks to warm them up."

"I get that. Connecting with the earth directly, feeling the difference in temperature," responded Pan. "Do you have boots with you though? I wouldn't advise buying new ones and then going for a walk where we are going."

"Yeah, where we live in the UK, walking boots is a must. I will run back and get them, with my fluffy socks," I said sticking my tongue out playfully at my hubby.

"You two are funny. I like you both. You are most welcome to come with me. Be back here in 20, I need to sort out some supplies from the store. Why don't you come with me and get some supplies for the pair of you whilst she gets her boots. I can see you are wrapped up ready for the cold." Pan directed her comments at Hubby.

"Desert boy. Anything colder than 15 degrees celsius and I need my thermals," he laughed back.

I walked back to the hotel and took in the noticeable differences in the surroundings. Seeing it all in the daylight and with more locals around, I noticed the tourists, myself included, stood out like a sore thumb. That said when I said 'haloogikpin' the friendly smile spread across the locals faces, and the men tipped their hats to me, well those who were not wearing beanie hats; they just put their hand to their head in a gesture of respect. I liked it here. People had traditions, there was a gentlemanly aspect to the interactions, which no doubt many modern-day feminist vigilantes would be offended by. There was a community feel to the place, but also the underlying vibe of 'the company', and I started to understand some of the 'not spoken' words Pan had put out into the air.

There was a divide between the fisherman, the corporates and 'the rest' of the town. The ones who made everything run smoothly, whether that was the waitresses in the cafés serving the coffee on the run, or those in the local stores selling a variety of different provisions, or the mechanics that kept the trucks, boats and 4 x 4s on the move. There was something I couldn't quite put my finger on, but there was an energy I hadn't noticed yesterday when Hubby and I had arrived, or this morning when I had gone to the beach.

Inside the hotel room, it felt homely, warm and cosy, and as I put on my fluffy fisherman socks, I giggled to myself as I wiggled my toes into the warmth of the wool. Both Hubby and Pan had been right. I did like the sensation of my feet being free and then wrapped up in the hug of warmth my socks provided. Socks were good, and so was walking around in bare feet. Too much sock time and your feet don't get the air they need, and we all need a bit of air to breathe. With this thought my mind went back to Pandora and her freediving. I was fascinated. I watched as the second hand on my watch hit the quarter past mark, then I held my breath. How long could I hold my breath? 30 seconds passed, one minute passed... 1:23 ... then I had to breathe. I laughed at the time... I could have got a Dusty Bin memento from Ted Rodgers for that in the UK! Bonus! Wouldn't have got me far in the water though... and if I had to go deep under the water, that would reduce the amount of time I could hold my breath because of the pressure of the water.

Looking at my watch again, I had to get back to the café so we could all head off on this adventure, whatever and wherever we were going. My mind drifted back to the idea of freediving and I tried holding my breath on the way back to the café. If I could hold my breath for two minutes on land, then what was that? One minute underwater? I was getting excited. Being underwater, free to move around without all that equipment, just me and the ocean… yeah, that sounded like a plan; but here? In Alaska? Yeah, no. That wasn't a plan. Not in any vision I could create in my mind… but… I bet the marine life here was mental. Hmmm… my mind started whirring and as soon as Hubby saw me he knew what I had been thinking.

"How long have you held your breath for then?" he asked laughing.

"I am up to almost two minutes so far," I replied.

"That's not too bad for a beginner," replied Pan.

"I am surprised it isn't more knowing how much she loves being in the water and how determined she is," answered Hubby.

"Well if she is really interested in taking up freediving there are lots of people around the world who she can learn from," Pan said before going on to hurry us into her truck. "Let's go," and off we went, no idea where we were going. We were just going off with this woman who I had met that morning, into the distance.

FOUR

TERRORS OF THE NIGHT

"So what time do you think we will be back at the hotel?" asked Hubby.

Pan laughed, a really hearty laugh. "Tonight? We won't be back for a couple of days. You're on Alaska time now my friend!"

"I am guessing that is a bit like Arab time Babe," I laughed, staring out of the window of the Jeep, hypnotised by the beauty of the snow-capped mountains and the glistening trees. It all sounded so cliché in my head, but I couldn't take my eyes off what was in front of me; if there was more of this, I would be happy to be gone for weeks, not just days.

"You're not worried about spending days with someone you have only just met, heading off into the distance, are you?" asked Pan.

"If she trusts you, then I'm fine with it."

"That's what I was thinking about you. Remember, it was her energy I connected with not yours, and if she married you, then you must be okay."

"She's trusts a bit too much if I am honest with you, but this is the raver way, the Arab way, and her way. Sometimes she goes off for hours, days even just doing her own thing. At first it used to worry me, but I know it is just her way. She needs time by herself." Hubby told Pan.

"I understand that," said Pan thoughtfully.

I wanted to let them both know I could hear what they were saying, but they knew I could hear them on some level. But then I couldn't, they seemed to drift off in the distance as I was looking out at the landscape, so beautiful, so silent, and so peaceful. I was with them, but I wasn't, and I was fine with that.

"We're just going to make another stop. There is someone I want you to meet," said Pan as she got out of the truck.

"You okay in the back there, Babe?" asked Hubby.

"I am more than okay. This landscape is just beautiful. Wish I had brought my ice skates, because I bet there are some amazing lakes around here to skate on."

"Yeah, I can imagine you now flying across the ice," he smiled to himself and I caught sight of it as I took my eyes off the landscape for just a moment to look at him. He really was a handsome man, with a deep kindness about him. Many misunderstood him, but I knew under that fierce persona he projected was a shy, peace-loving person who just wanted fairness, respect and justice in the world. He had a big heart, and it had been battered many times by his mother whilst growing up. He protected her fiercely, but she hurt him over and over with her nasty criticisms. He was a truly generous and open soul, but had learnt to hide himself away, to shut himself down. I felt very blessed to be his wife, the one he had chosen to open up his heart to, his mind and his goals for the future. Sometimes I wondered how I had gotten so lucky, but I knew luck had nothing to do with it. We were soul mates, contracted through lifetimes to be together to fulfil a purpose neither of us knew. And even though he didn't believe in 'all that stuff' he accepted it was something that I did believe in.

The door opened, and I felt it. He felt it, they felt it. That power surge which many around the world who watched action movies would describe as an electromagnetic pulse. It was powerful, and I felt as though I had been stunned with this energy force, almost winded to the point of passing out.

"Moana, meet Nuliajuk, and her husband Abdu. They will be traveling with us."

Nuliajuk climbed into the back of the truck with me. There were no words needed. Nuliajuk's eyes locked on mine and we knew. We knew we were from another time and place together, destined to meet again in another lifetime and here we were. I was feeling like I was in a dream, like I was floating.

"Shegh nununyu," Nuliajuk smiled.

"I did," and we embraced. A flood of emotions rose within me and I felt like a lifetime of worries had just fallen away in a moment.

"So you two know each other then?" asked Pan.

"We do," we both answered together, holding each other's hands, one overlaying the other.

Abdu sat there, not sure what to make of it all.

"Right then, Ugha! Let's go!"

"You've got to love it when no translation is needed,"

said Abdu, as we all sat there processing everything that had just happened in a split second.

We continued the drive west and the landscape was just as spectacular as the moments before, unrelenting in the majestic beauty of it all. The day seemed as never ending as the beauty of the landscapes, and I noticed Abdu had fallen asleep. I was feeling tired, and almost as I thought about tiredness, Nuliajuk placed her hand on Pan's shoulder, and Pan pulled over.

"Right then, time to get ready for the night ahead." Pan jumped out of the truck, and Abdu slowly woke up. Nuliajuk and I got out of the truck and went off to find firewood together. No words had been spoken verbally but the conversation was flowing through us uninterrupted. Smiles, nods, hands being held tighter, breathing quickening and slowing.

Pan was fascinated by what she was seeing, but obviously not surprised. It was the way it was. Normal. It is why we were all here, and this wasn't about me or Nuliajuk; both of us knew that. This was about Pan, this was to be her journey, and we were to witness whatever was to come up for her with our union.

Returning back to the truck, I noticed for the first time a small wooden cabin, the kind I had always imagined I would see in the Canadian outback, except this wasn't Canada, this was land stolen by America, and if we went back far enough, Russia. The cabin had a small wood burner and chimney, with six camp beds folded in the corner. Plenty of blankets, six enamel cups and a couple of saucepans, and a stove top pot for boiling water. There was some cured meat in the corner and plenty of onions and potatoes. It was as if the cabin had been stocked for our arrival.

"It is always stocked for travellers passing through," said Pan as she pulled out a bed for Abdu, who was strangely still sleepy.

"Are you okay, Babe?" I asked, knowing on a deeper level this was as it should be. He was not to be part of the evening events. He was simply travelling in the physical realm, and for us women, we would be travelling into a different world, through a different realm of existence.

"Yeah, I am just really tired. I am going to go to sleep. Enjoy your evening together, and I will see you in the morning," and with that he kissed me on the forehead and climbed into the unfolded camp bed, pulled one of the fur blankets over him, taking a moment to notice the softness and the heaviness of it, before pulling it right up to his chin and falling straight to sleep again.

Pan had already started to make coffee, and Nuliajuk had gotten the fire ready outside the cabin. The sky was still light and wouldn't be dark for long when the light did disappear. I had no idea of time and didn't care. I sat down on the log by the fire, everything seeming to be where I needed it to be when I needed it to be there. I loved this kind of magic, and I loved the flow state of just being. The smell of fresh coffee filled the air, with fresh pine from the fire. Hmmm the smell of a fire, fresh coffee and the crackling of the wood burning in front of me, with the backdrop of the white snowy landscape. I felt like I was dreaming, and in some ways I was. I was not in the world I had woken up in that morning. This was a different realm and it needed to be, because there was work to done.

Nuliajuk and I sat opposite each other, looking into the fire and our breathing synchronised. Slow, deep and intentional. Pan walked over to the fire and sat on the log to my right, next to Nuliajuk. She knew, we knew she knew. We all knew. There were no accidents or coincidences in life. Every meeting was a meeting that needed to happen, for knowledge or healing to take place, and this night it was time for Pan to travel through something that she had been avoiding, numbing and locking out in the cold. She had been holding her breath for far too long pretending all was good, but deep down that anger I had sensed over breakfast with her was stopping her from moving forward, Meeting Nuliajuk, I knew in that powerful moment when our souls met in human form, we were going to visit all those moments which had stolen Pan's breath, placed an ice core inside of her and were going to bring them to the surface so she could release them once and for all. They were not hers to hold onto, they were not hers to carry, and this wasn't about return to sender, this was about burning them in the fire and alchemising them.

***

There was no 'official beginning' to the evening's work, it just began with Nuliajuk whispering a song into the air, and then Pan and I joining her. I didn't know these words, but my soul did. They came from within me as easily as the air needed to breathe. Nuliajuk looked at me and I knew it was time. Pulling out a seal skin pouch, Nuliajuk took out a vial of oil, and a smaller pouch of what looked like mixed herbs. She threw those on the fire and rubbed the oil into her hands, placed her hands over her face, and then repeated the process with Pan, and then me. The smell of berries and pine filled my nostrils, invoking a sense of calmness and being cleansed.

We were sat by a fire, in the cold night air, and the combination of heat and wind burn, it made sense to have the moisture of an oil to protect the skin. I had no real knowledge of what was in the herbs, or in the oil, but the combination of the two made perfect sense to me on an unconscious level. The herbs to relax us and the oil to protect our skin from the combination of heat and ice-cold air, burns of polarity prevented with the simplicity and complexity of nature.

After a few moments, we were on a completely different plain of existence, and deeply buried memories were being shared between us from deep within Pan's consciousness. I could see them as clearly as if I were watching them being played out on a TV screen.

Lying there in her bed, her blanket pulled up to her chin, as if to create a protective seal so nothing could get in; that's when her eyes widen in fear, the terror of that noise she had just heard. He was on the other side of the door, about to come in and take what was not his to take, but in his arrogance and sense of self-righteousness, he would take anyway. The door opened and there he was, the man she feared most in the world, but the one she obeyed the most. The one who had a control over her like no one else. The one who they all adored, cheered and wanted to be around. The one she hated and wanted to run from. The one who had taught her that she could not trust her own body, and if she could not trust her own body, how could she trust herself?

"Hello Pandora," he whispered, "How are you? Are you ready to play?" His smile excited, and his eyes dancing at the sight of her laying there in fear. He turned and closed the door, and the room filled with the scent of his desire, her fear and the expensive aftershave he favoured. "Don't be afraid of me, I am not going to hurt you. We are going to have fun, like we always do. You know you like the way our fun makes you feel. Your body wouldn't lie to you my angel. All that wetness that comes from within you is a sign you like it, and I wouldn't fit inside you if I wasn't meant to. We are a perfect fit you and I. Don't be afraid."

He started to unbutton his shirt in front of her as if she were his willing lover, instead of a paralysed prisoner. "You know, I have been thinking of you all day. You've been a major distraction during all my meetings, but my greatest inspiration all at once." He was now unbuttoning his fly, and she lay there terrified. She could feel herself tightening down below but throbbing all at the same time. He was right, she couldn't trust her body. If she was really truly afraid of him, and he wasn't meant to be here with her doing all these things, then why did her body react like this?

He came closer to her. She gripped the bedding even tighter, and then as he reached up over her to the cupboard above her bed. His muscly body, tight and strong, obscuring her view of everything, and she saw he was already hard for her. "Ah there it is, 'Pandora's Box'." He laughed at his own words. "Are you ready my darling?"

He lay down on the big double bed beside her. Her fear intensified but so did her curiosity of what he would do to her tonight. How long would he play with her? What would it feel like tonight? Would she remember it in the morning? Would she feel pain tomorrow? So many questions racing through her mind, trying to outrun the fear, wishing she could move, but as always she was paralysed. She couldn't move anything. She never could, all she could do was lay there and watch from another place in her mind as he moved her into whatever position he wanted her to. At first he uncurled her fingers from the bedding. "You don't need to hold onto that Pandora, hold this instead," he said with yet another laugh to himself as he moved her small hand around his hard cock, wrapping her delicate fingers around it and moving her hand up and down. She had no control over her body; he could do to her what he liked. "Ah yes, just what I have been looking forward to all day," he said as he moved his groin slowly up and down, his cock held by her small hand and his hand over hers. He was trapped by her, and she was trapped by him, locked together, her in fear and him in pleasure. "Oh Pandora, if only you knew what you do to me."

She closed her eyes, her eyelids the only thing she could move, and then she was gone deep into that place she took herself to, the place where he couldn't get to her, until he changed to the next game.

The wind was howling, and the fire was raging, screaming along with the internal screams of Pan. She was now on the fur rug beside the fire with Nuliajuk and I either side of her. I was holding her left hand, with Nuliajuk holding her own hands above Pan's body. The night sky was still light, and the desolateness of the area meant we were the only ones around, other than the animals and birds in the woodlands which surrounded us. I felt a calmness and a oneness I had never felt before and was not unnerved by what I was witnessing. It felt a little like the nights Abdu and I had explored each other's mind when we had taken acid together, but this experience was cleaner, purer and the journey was more lucid. Although what I was witnessing in the depths of Pan's unconscious was incredibly unpleasant, I felt detached from the terror and the fear, the pain and the evil. It was passing in front of me, and as it left her, I filled her with the love that flowed through me. I felt as though I was watching all of this take place in front of me, but I was also deep within it, whilst also being able to check that Abdu was still sleeping without actually moving. I was in all three spaces at the same time, where I needed to be for everyone to be taken care of.

The wind started to howl even louder, and I was taken back into the depths of Pan's memories, ready for her to release herself from them one final time so she could move on for good.

Thrusting himself inside of her, her small body responding against her wishes, betraying her with every pulse of the orgasm that her body delivered, he delighted in her body's pleasure. "See, you do enjoy this Pandora, you know this is right… and this…" he moved one of his hands which were pinning her arms above her head and pulled out a 'new toy from Pandora's box'… "You will like this too." He didn't show her what it was he had just taken from 'her box', he just withdrew himself and inserted it inside her, both back and front, before inserting himself inside her with it. He let out a yelp of desire as he switched on the power of his new toy and she let out a noise of fear and physical pleasure all at the same time.

Inside she was crying, but yet again her body was betraying her. She wanted to scream, kick and punch him away, but other than the movements he made with her body, there was nothing she could do. She couldn't even move the arms he had pinned above her head, he just liked pinning her down.

The look of pleasure on his face, the joy he was experiencing playing with her and his 'new toy' made her want to be sick, but the feelings she was experiencing in other parts of her body took over. "I knew we would enjoy this together; I knew it would bring us both so much pleasure. Look at all the juices you have produced Pandora. Such a woman you are, and at such a young age."

In that moment something within her changed, a death had just occurred and the feeling of being icy cold enveloped her. She felt her body surrender and go limp.

There was nothing more left within her to torture and she left his world behind.

The images disintegrated, fracturing and dissolving into the night air. Pan's body went limp, forcing a dark smoke like breath to leave her body. In that instant, the frown across her forehead softened. She looked almost childlike in her peace, and her breathing returned to normal.

I watched as Nuliajuk moved her hands over Pan's body, stopping above her groin, and then moving her hands in a scooping like motion as if removing something. I then saw myself add more wood to the fire, with a sprinkle of the herbs from Nuliajuk's pouch. I took a deep breath, noticing Nuliajuk did the same, and as I moved back to Pan's side, her body came alive with a big gasp of air. Her eyes opened but were still closed to the physical world. She was still under the influence of the herbs and deep in the world of releasing the trauma she had experienced as a young girl.

Her breathing quickened and the images started forming again in our combined consciousness. This time she was older and sat with a woman who I knew to be her mother before needing an introduction.

"I don't want to go. You don't want to go, so why do we have to go?" cried Pandora to her mother.

"Because if we don't then he will be cross with us, and

it won't look good. This is a big event for the family Pandora, and we have to go," answered her mother in her usual quiet, almost silent manner.

"You hate these events, we hate him, why can't we just stay home?" pleaded Pandora.

"Please don't use that word Pandora. It is a bad word, and if it weren't for him, we wouldn't have the life we have. Daddy wouldn't have a job, and we wouldn't have the home, clothes and opportunities we have," reminded her mother, as much to herself as to her daughter.

"I don't care about any of these things. I don't like going to his parties with his friends, all the cameras and all these people. I just want to stay in my room or make a cake with you. Mama please?"

"Pandora, please stop your pleading. You know this is a big night for everyone at the company, and your dad. There are not many good jobs around here, and Daddy needs this job," stated her mother as firmly as a frightened mouse, like her mother could do.

"Why do you do this? You hate him as much as I do. You know you hate being around people, and yet you always do what he tells you to do. You're afraid of him… aren't you?" Pandora said looking her mother directly in the eyes, and just before her mother could drop her gaze, Pandora saw the fear, the terror and knew, she knew she was not the only one. He had done it to her mother too.

Pandora ran from the room, the nausea rising inside of her, the ground falling away from her feet, her legs feeling like jelly and before she could get to the bathroom, she threw up everywhere. How could he do this to his own sister? And how long had it been going on? His own sister?

And her daughter? His niece. Both of them. The sickness rose up again and she threw up again, and again. The more she connected the dots, the more she threw up. This is why her mother was so quiet, so timid, so subservient to him. She was terrified of him for the same reasons she was. And her dad worked for him! Her small body emptied itself again and she collapsed onto the floor weak from the power of the realisations.

Her mother came to her with a glass of water, and a cold compress for her head. "Pandora, you must be strong. We mustn't upset him, because it will get worse if we do. Just stay close to me and Daddy and everything will be alright. He will protect us; you know he always does. Now come on, drink this, wipe your face and let's get ready. And remember, stay close to Daddy and I."

Pandora could see the fear in her mother's eyes, the pleading for her to not make a fuss, not tonight. This was the biggest night in the company's history so far, according to the snippets of conversation Pandora had overheard. There had been meetings long into the night which had saved her from more nights of terror with him, and for that she had been relieved. She wanted the family business to be a huge success if it meant he stayed away from her. She would play her part, she would get dressed, she would go to this stupid party and she would stay so close to her mother and father it would be as if they were wearing an invisible cloaking device. She wouldn't leave her father's side, and she certainly wouldn't go anywhere near him. With that final thought of being near him she threw up once more, this time the lining of her stomach came with the remnants of whatever was left.

Pan's body was convulsing each and every time the memories of vomiting ripped through her body, and with each convulsion, more dark smoke left her mouth as it mimicked the action of being sick. This was a deep purging, and although I had never been witness to this before, not that I could remember in this lifetime, I knew that these were the residual elements buried deep within the layers of Pan's subconscious. I was fascinated and yet not surprised. I knew what to expect, and yet had no expectations. I had taken hallucinogens with Abdu before to go deep into aspects of our minds, to explore subjects and to heighten the sensations of the body, but this was a whole new level of expanded consciousness, and yet I had been here before. I had done this before, and I had done it with Nuliajuk, this is why we had all felt that intense connection earlier in the day.

I had no answers for any of this work. I didn't even begin to try and figure it out, it was just what it was. If someone had told me in the morning I would be here in the middle of a beautiful snowy landscape, knelt by a complete strangers body, next to a fire doing this kind of healing work, whilst my husband lay asleep in the cabin behind us, I would have looked at them as if they were off their rocker.

I didn't do hallucinogens with anyone I didn't know. To go deep into the mind with people you didn't know I believed to be stupid. You didn't know what they could do to your consciousness, and yet here I was, having gotten into a truck with a woman who had appeared out of the ocean that morning, ice cold water at that, the first full day of a holiday in a country I had never been to before, going deep into sacred parts of her subconsciousness with a shamanic medicine woman, who I had known, and recognised on sight, from lifetimes before.

Had I inhaled too much of these herbs? Was I still dreaming and would wake up in the hotel room having never gone to the beach that morning? All of these thoughts started going through my mind, and then I felt Nuliajuk's hand on my hand; I knew everything was as it was meant to be, and I was to leave my own mind and return to the work we were doing with Pan.

This was her journey, not mine, and I had to leave the physical world and return to the higher levels of consciousness.

FIVE

IN PLAIN SIGHT

Seeing her name in my inbox, a smile spread across my face. Forgetting all work emails, I opened up the email, I was looking forward to reading how Pan had been getting on. It had been years since that incredible night in Alaska by the fire with Nuliajuk.

Do you remember that night we first met? Pretty intense to say the least. I have been feeling a bit weird about how it all happened and how you didn't know me or Nuliajuk, but still you went deep into my healing journey with us both. Who does that? Who gets in truck with someone they don't know and goes on this mad crazy journey with someone and doesn't even bat an eyelid? I didn't think you were a nutter to be honest with you, but over time I have realised you're pretty special, you do know that right? But you probably don't, and even if people have told you, you probably accept it with that cute smile of yours and thank them, before moving onto the next topic of conversation. I can see you smiling to yourself now, because I know I am right. Anyway, if you are not aware of just how special you are, and I hope you do, I just want to say that even though we went deep together, I never really got to tell you how truly grateful I am for what you did for me that night. You never judged me for what you witnessed in my fucked-up world, and even if you did, you didn't show it. Honestly, and please believe me, I never expected any of that to happen, well not until you and Nuliajuk met. Man, that was an intense moment. I would ask what the fuck that was, but knowing Nuiajuk, and seeing how you two connected I know it was one of those 'ancestor' moments she speaks of.

Not sure if you know, but her name means 'woman with a fin, who is leader of all the seals in the sea'… and what with you being the mermaid you are, not surprised there is some ancient shaman stuff going on between you. Hell, you might even both be seal leaders together! I can imagine you now, both of you doing some pretty insane stuff together in the ocean. She needs healing you know, the ocean. Seriously, if you saw the stuff I saw down there when I am diving, you wouldn't be happy. I know you love the ocean more than most normal people, and don't worry, not putting you in the normal bracket, but I think you would cry. The amount of trash down there, or as you Brits like to say 'rubbish' – makes me angry but can't do that whilst I am down there... I save that for later when moaning in the café. Noah says hi by the way, asks if I had heard from you. It's thanks to him actually that I am writing to you. He keeps telling me to write to you, let you know if you ever want to eat happy animals again, he'll go out and shoot a reindeer for you. Funny the impact you had on people here to be honest, like when you left, we all felt it. When are you coming back? Are *you ever going to come back? Or did my crazy put you off? I don't think so, you wouldn't have given me this email address otherwise, would you? Got to stop doubting myself and doubting that you actually do like me. Still have problems with that you know. Look at me, chatting away to you as if you are here with me having a coffee – which by the way, I now make in a coffee pot on the stove like you taught me 'Arabic styleee'. Makes me smile every time I say that. Haha! So why am I writing to you? Well, other than to find out how you are, I'm finally ready to answer that question you asked me to ask myself, or should I say, I am finally ready to share with you what the answer was to the question you asked me, which as you can probably tell, I have avoided like an oil slick in the ocean.*

You may not even remember the question, but this is what you asked me: "If you stay quiet, knowing what you know, and you find out he does it to another person, will you be able to live with those feelings, knowing you could have done something to prevent it?"

A pretty fucking loaded question Moana! What the fuck!? Nothing like giving a person something to think about and make them choose to be part of the problem or part of the solution!

I will be honest, you pissed me off with that question. Like REALLY pissed me off! If you do ever come back here, you can ask Noah, I sulked around the place for ages, dived deeper and for longer than ever, so in some ways I have a lot to thank you for, because if nothing else my diving improved. Noah even threatened to ban me from the café! Can you believe that!? You probably can actually. He knew you had something to do with my mood, and I knew I had to process it. So what did I do? I did your trick; you know your Crocodile Dundee trick of 'going walkabout'. Yeah, Abdu told me all about the times you would just disappear for a walk for hours or disappear off to the beach for some alone time. You know I really do hope by now you have taken up diving. Okay, so it's not really one of those Mick Dundee walkabouts but still, I did go Mick Dundee. Disappeared for weeks. People started to worry and when I got back to Bethel, I got a massive telling off by my mate Hunter, and word had spread back to Anchorage that I hadn't been seen for weeks. Noah lost it with me, threatened to kill me himself next time I went off for walk without telling him. "Could have given you some bloody sausages to keep your strength up!" Those bloody sausages of his! I'm telling you, on his gravestone it will read "Here lies Noah, maker of the finest reindeer sausages in the Northern Hemisphere, which he served with light fluffy waffles and eggs from the chickens out back."

Reading this email, I was transported back to Anchorage and the smell of those sausages and waffles, Noah's hearty laugh and his Uncle persona to everyone. I smiled from deep within and liked how Pan's email just flowed. She was in a good place, I could tell, and I could almost feel her punch me in the arm for asking her that question. I did remember asking her it, and I am glad she took the time to think about it before answering it. Intrigued to find out what her answer was, I checked to see how much longer the email was. I had a lot of work to do, my dog to walk and I knew that if the email flowed as much as this, and she kept avoiding the answer by filling me in with all the news of meanings of names, and Noah and his sausages, she was going to avoid getting to the answer. I had a meeting to get to and knowing how deep we have gone into her subconscious that first night, then I would be no good to anyone in the meeting. Scrolling the length of the email, it was a long one, and that was even by my standards. I parked the email, walked my dog and then came back and prepped for the meeting, my mind wandering back to the morning after the night of the fire.

"What time is it?" I asked.

"You mean you can't tell by looking at the sky?" teased Pan gently.

"Your daylight hours are crazy here, and do you still call them daylight hours, when we are in the night? Or is night just a word for the dark? Hmmm never considered that before…" my mid wandered.

"Look at you with your after-herb musings," Pan teased again, this time with a post deep healing nervousness.

"How are you feeling? You went really deep, and lots came up for you. You must be shattered."

"I don't remember much to be honest, but I know I feel lighter, clearer. Like a weight, a pressure has been taken away from me. Like when I come up from the depths of the ocean. Like I've been rebirthed," Pan shared quietly.

Nuliajuk was quietly making coffee and watching Pan with care, who had just gone incredibly deep into memories and emotions buried and not dealt with. She was also making a separate drink in a different pot, one that had almost magically appeared out of nowhere.

Whatever it was that was going into this herbal mix smelled so refreshing and even smelling it, I felt clean from the inside out. Juniper. Was that even a berry in these parts?

Watching Nuliajuk was mesmerising. She was an ancient, with a strong energy and just being in her space was powerful. She moved slowly, purposefully and with a grace like nothing I had ever witnessed in a woman of her age… which, to be honest, I had no idea of what that would be. Human years she was easily passed seventy; soul wise, she was millennia, through times of intense suffering and enlightenment, and yet here she was as peaceful as the place we were sitting in. She didn't look physically tired, but she was tired of this world, and I had a feeling this would be the only time we would meet in this lifetime, but we had many more healings to do in lifetimes to come. She looked up at me and nodded, as if she could read my thoughts, and of course she could. What we had just done with Pan, and the journey of combined consciousness, of course she could read my thoughts and my energy.

I was tired. I hadn't experienced this kind of journey before, not like this. Taking acid with someone you love and trust, just going off on a journey of the mind was one thing, inhaling shamanic herbs with a shaman with complete strangers and going deep into a trauma healing… yeah, slightly different.

"So, that was intense…" offered Pan.

"You could say that," I replied.

"Are you okay?" she asked me.

"Yeah, I am fine, slightly tired, but mostly honoured that you trusted me with this journey of yours."

"Trust me, I had no idea any of this was going to happen; but when Nuliajuk enters your world, you just go with it. Don't you, Nuliajuk?"

"It is not me Pan; it is the Spirits above who brought us together so we could heal this darkness within you; within all of us. This is not your pain alone Pan. We are souls connected through lifetimes, through experiences, and we must work together to heal one another. When we are called we are called, and there is nothing we can do to prevent it. We can delay it, but it will always find a way to reveal itself." Nuliajuk handed both Pan and I a cup of coffee each.

"So, if I had not arrived here in Alaska, then this would have taken place somewhere else?" I asked.

"Of course, that is how things work. Maybe this lifetime together, maybe in a different place, with us in different forms, but it would have happened. It is written. It is all written," said Nuliajuk as she walked back to her side of the fire and drank the other liquid she had been making.

Both Pan and I sat there deep in thought, before she broke the silence.

"You know that night, the night I realised what he had done to my mum, I began to understand why she had always been like a timid little mouse, never leaving the house, and flinching whenever men came near her. I used to think my dad was really possessive, controlling, but after I had time to process everything I realised he was just being protective of her. He never left her side, would never allow her to work in the company, and I always thought he was stopping her, like he was some kind of old-fashioned husband who thought the woman's place was in the home.

"Dad was always so gentle with my mum. They were childhood friends you know. Mum trusted him without question, and I have always wondered why Dad worked at the firm. Was it to keep an eye on things, to make sure Mum's inheritance wasn't squandered, or to make sure *he* didn't go near her. I never did find out before they died in the crash. I was relieved for Mum when she died. I knew she no longer had to see him, or relive what he did to us, not just physically but as mother and daughter. That level of betrayal, that division he had over us, the way he manipulated our bond as parent and child. He robbed us of something which could have been so beautiful.

"I went to the party you know, and I started to notice things which made me realise mum and I were not the only ones. I saw waitresses avoid serving him, women who worked in the company keep their distance from him and those who were laughing would stop and start looking uncomfortable when he was in their presence. I was only 14 but I could tell who he had been raping and abusing, and some of them reminded me of Mum: quiet, reserved and timid. And it made me wonder how long he had been doing it to them.

"What really surprised me though was how others couldn't see it, and if they could, why they didn't put a stop to it, step in and protect us all, have him arrested. None of it made sense to me, so I went walking the next day, and I kept walking."

I sat and listened. Her voice had changed, her energy, she was calmer, less angry and as I looked up, I saw

Nuliajuk catch my eye and nod. I looked back to Pan, her gaze off into the distance, looking at the snow-covered pine trees surrounding us.

"It looked a lot like this you know, where I went walking. Canada is a beautiful country when you get away from the city of Vancouver. It's not that the city itself is ugly, or a bad place, but it wasn't a good place for me, for Mum. Everywhere I went in that city I would see his face, hear his voice. Radio, TV, billboards, newspapers, magazines… the city's superhero, the one who made the city what it was; but it wasn't. My grandfather and great uncle did. They built that company from the ground up over 'a whiskey and smoke one Sunday whilst out hunting' and he took all the credit. Everyone thought Mum just didn't have what it took to run the business, she was just too quiet, too 'mousey' but he took that from her. He made sure she didn't take her place in the boardroom, he made sure she never took what he thought was his by taking everything from her, even her trust in herself, and her body. Who does that?"

She went quiet, and I sat beside her just listening, holding space for her, looking at the trees and the skyline. It really was beautiful here.

"You know, that walk, that was where it happened you know. I had been walking for ages and been sleeping in the same clothes. I must have been gone for at least four days. That's when I came across this little lake. I looked around, collected some wood and made a fire and then stripped off and got in the water. I was a bit like you at first, hesitant about getting into the cold water, but I just kept walking, and then the ground was gone, and I was under the water.

I didn't panic, I actually thought, 'Good, it's over now,' and in some ways it was. The water was so cold, so clear and because it was so cold, my mind was soon focused on the cold rather than the thoughts which had been racing through my mind the past few days. The cold of the water numbed the pain of all the walking, and I remember the moment I thought to myself, 'If it can numb the pain of the walking… it can numb the pain of what he's done…' and so I stayed under the water, willingly embracing the ice-cold water, not wanting to leave it, wanting to stay there forever. But then something made me get out of the water. It was like a voice in my head telling me to get out. I don't know how long I had been in the water, but as I rose out of the water and the icy air hit my skin, it made me shudder, and it felt like something had fallen away from me, like I had shed a skin. There was a feeling of overcoming, and my mind was filled with new thoughts and I was so lost in thoughts I nearly walked into the fire I had built before going in. Sitting by the fire, next to my clothes, I could feel the heat of the flames, but I didn't want to move. It was like I had been numb all my life and the ice had awakened something in me and now the fire was intensifying it. So I took my clothes back to the water, washed them and then after I had done that I hung them over the branches of the trees nearby whilst I sat by the fire. I was totally naked, and it didn't bother me. For the first time since he visited me in that room at night, I felt that I could trust my body. I remember sitting there and crying, and the next thing I knew Nuliajuk was there beside me and there was a fur blanket over me. The fire was burning with fresh wood and my clothes were dry. It was the first time we met, and she's always been there when I needed her."

I looked around and realised that Nuliajuk had gone, like she had never been there. Gone without a trace, and yet she had left something so powerful behind in both Pan and I.

An awakening had taken place in both of us, and I was reminded of the first time I took acid with Abdu. The images I would see, the colours and the depth of our conversations, all so beautifully powerful. We didn't take acid like everyone else we knew, those who took it just to get wasted. We took it with purpose, for discovery and I loved it. I had always seen auras ever since I was a young girl and taking acid had opened up a portal in my being that allowed me to see energy and auras on a whole new level. One of the reasons I loved being by myself is because the energy was lighter, more magical, purer on so many levels. Going out raving and losing myself on the dancefloor, getting lost and carried away in the music, I would visit places in my mind, and it was like I became part of the music. There was no end and no beginning, we, I, were just being, as one energy form, molecules dancing through space together. It felt so beautiful and because there were no words, there was no pollution of thought. Words in songs messed with my mojo. I just wanted the heartbeat of music, the heartbeat of the energy of the moment.

For Pan, the awakening was different. Her awakening was the revelation of letting go, of gaining peace, releasing all that had been bottled up within her, and now she was pouring out through her voice the words which had been like a hand around her throat, strangling her for years.

I turned back to her and she was still looking out into the distance, but this time she was not looking at the trees, she was looking beyond the trees, beyond this realm, that ten thousand mile stare into the atmosphere beyond anyone else's comprehension, into her own world. She had left the world of pain behind and was now in a new world of ultimate possibilities, a parallel universe, one where she could now create whatever she wanted, absorbing new energies, living into a new existence which had always been hers, but one which had been locked away in the limited consciousness of before.

SIX

ICE COLD SERENITY

"It was so silent under the water, like I was drowning out the voices, the screams in my own head, which never made it out of my mouth. I never felt like I was drowning, I just felt at peace when I was under the water. I'd never felt that before, not that I could remember anyway. No one telling me off for being quiet, no one telling me how to be, no one telling me to just 'snap out of it'… like they knew what I was dealing with. I mean, what could possibly be wrong in my life? My family had millions, were always on the invite list to all the best social parties and I was just the ungrateful brat that didn't appreciate it, according to many." There was a sense of melancholy in her voice, but no resentment. It was all gone, here in this moment anyway. The edge to her voice was gone, and all that remained was a softness, and a renewed sense of courage.

I got up and added a few more little bits of wood to the fire, just to spark it up again. I was getting cold, and Pan was deep in sharing mode. Neither of us were tired, which was surprising to be honest. I mean, I had no idea how long we had been under the influence of the herbs, and the night sky, if that is what you could call it, was still light. How did people tell the time here? I looked around and saw the moon at about 22 degrees above the earth's surface which could have meant anything really. This was only my second night in Alaska, my first night out in 'the wilds' and I guessed it was probably around 4 am. But as someone who never wore a watch, or bothered with time when not working, I was happy to just be sat by the fire.

"You know what Moana, I can't help but wonder what made him the way he is. Did someone do this to him? How did he learn to be this way? I mean, no one is born this evil, surely? I just feel sad for him now, and most of all I feel sad for my mum, and for me. He robbed himself of a sister who was a really smart woman, he robbed her of an amazing life, and he robbed me of my mum, and my dad of a relationship with his daughter; because I never allowed my dad to get close to me. I don't remember a time he didn't do those things to me. I don't remember a time when I didn't know he was coming, I could smell that aftershave of his. How can people take so much from so many people, and then go out into the world and pretend to be the good guy, the one who smiles and laughs with so many people, being the community hero? He must be one of those people who can switch off a part of themselves and not know about who he is, like a split personality. Or he just loved the fact he could get away with it and that is what the laughter was all about, the way he could fool so many people. What do you think?"

"To be honest with you Pan, I don't think people like us are meant to understand people like that. It just isn't something we could compute or comprehend for a variety of different reasons. We can ask what made them that way, but in all honesty, when we become adults if we choose to continue to make choices on what was done to us, instead of making choices which make us better people, then we are not being adult. We are choosing not to become better people, and I think that is a waste of a life. Does that mean we are free of making mistakes? Not at all, but we can't blame what happened in our childhood or what happened to us in our past when we are conscious beings. We get to choose in every moment to do the right thing, and that right thing will evolve the more we evolve and learn about ourselves. The sad thing is though, so many people don't want to learn and evolve, they just want to numb their pain with TV, toxic food and gossip about others. It makes them forget their own problems and that's what the higher echelons of society and big pharma want, customers of pain and suffering, it keeps them in control and in business."

Pan looked at me. "I'd never thought about it like that before." She stared off into the distance.

I could tell she was starting to feel really tired, and so was I. "Come on, let's go to the cabin, I think we could both do with some sleep. You, my lovely, have had one hell of a journey tonight. Thank you for trusting me with your journey." I held my hand out to her, she took it and pulled herself up. She moved slowly, like she was in a daze, and we linked arms as we headed back towards the cabin. I looked at the fire and the twigs I'd added had done their job, with the embers left in the base of the fire glowing nicely. With the amount of snow on the ground and the distance from the trees there was no way anything would catch fire; the fire would keep ready for us to spark it up again in a few hours for cooking breakfast and making that all important pot of coffee when we woke up. Abdu would be awake in a few hours, so getting some sleep was essential. We couldn't really let him be awake all by himself out here in the middle of nowhere with no one to speak with after we had journeyed through the realms of another world.

Opening the door of the cabin, the warmth of the wood burner intensified the feelings of tiredness, and I was thankful we had unfolded the camp beds before going out to be by the fire with Nuliajuk. The fur blankets were heavy and warm and as we wished each other sweet dreams, I really did hope that on this night at least, Pan's mind would be clear of any unpleasant memories. I looked over at Abdu, and he was in his own deep sleep. I wondered if he had been gifted a sleep aid by Nuliajuk to make sure he stayed asleep but knowing how hard he had been working before we came away, and knowing how much we both needed this holiday, I knew he didn't need anything to help him sleep for hours. I pulled the blanket up close to my chin, thanked God for my blessings and fell into a deep sleep.

Waking up, both Pan and I were more refreshed than we thought we would be. Abdu had already got the coffee on the go and hadn't been awake very long himself.

"What time did you two come to bed? I'm sorry I

crashed and burned so quickly last night, but by the looks of it, you had a good night by the fire."

"No idea what time we came to bed. It was such a beautiful evening in so many ways, we just stayed awake talking and going off on one," replied Pan.

"Bet there was a rabbit hole or two thrown into that conversation, knowing you Babe," Abdu said, looking straight at me.

"Oh you know, one or two," I answered with a smile and a giggle at Pan.

"Oh I see, whilst the men sleep and all that…" teased Abdu.

"Yeah we were dancing naked around the fire, taking hallucinogens and everything! It was amazing!" I laughed back at him.

"With you, I wouldn't be surprised. Except it would be a bit cold wouldn't it for naked dancing?" laughed Abdu.

"Not with a fire you muppet! Tsk! All hot and cold all at the same time… that pleasure pain thing you know," I laughed.

Pan didn't quite know what to say, so just stood there and giggled away to herself, shaking her head. "You two are nuts."

"Yeah, it's why he loves me," I laughed as I danced around the fire, arms in the air, almost skipping and then throwing myself on the floor to make a snow angel… not that there was much snow, but there was enough.

"So Pan, you said yesterday you do this freediving. What's it like?" asked Abdu.

"Honestly?"

"No, I want you to lie to me," Abdu joked with her.

"You're funny. It is just one of those things that unless you do it, or have done any kind of underwater swimming, you just can't explain it. It's like nothing I have ever done before," said Pan as she started to look off into the tress like she had done the night before. "Have you ever done any diving before?"

"I tried it once, but I couldn't equalise," replied Abdu.

"Underwater swimming?" asked Pan.

I nearly choked on my coffee and snorted it out through my nose. "Sorry didn't mean to laugh and snort at that, but just couldn't help it."

"I take it you are not a strong swimmer then Abdu?"

"I am not any kind of swimmer, unless you call panicking because the water is chest high as you walk out into the ocean swimming," laughed Abdu at himself. "She's the swimmer, or rather the dolphin and mermaid. Put her in the water, on the water – liquid or frozen, and she's as happy as you like."

Pan looked at me, and I smiled back at her. "Okay, well, the first time I did any kind of freediving, was the kind most people do when they try and swim a 25 metre length of a pool underwater without coming up for air…" Pan noticed the look on Abdu's face, "Which I am guessing you have never done, by that look."

"I don't think I have ever done even a metre underwater." Looking at me, he said, "Her though? She scares the life out of me sometimes. Under the water in the pool, the ocean, and staying under the surface even in the bath."

"Okay… so anyway. I started swimming as far as I could underwater and seeing how far I could go, and then

I started to try and keep to the floor of the pool. This was just normal kids stuff to me. But it was when I went walkabout and ended up in Porteau Cove, about a week's walk from where I lived near Vancouver, that the switch in my brain went on."

"A week's walk! You mean you walked non-stop for a week? Not surprised you got in some cold water, your legs and feet must have been killing you!" Abdu said shocked that any would walk that far.

"What I was walking from was killing me more," Pan replied reflecting on the memories, which didn't look as though they stung her as much as the day before. "When you first go into the cold water, it is a shock to the system, but as with anything, it is mind over matter."

"Like you say Babe, 'I don't mind, so the drugs don't matter'," Abdu reminded me.

Pan looked at me confused.

"What I mean by that Pan, is I don't mind the journey I am embarking with the drugs, or the comedown, so the impact doesn't matter in the sense of: I know I am responsible and have done my research on the effects, I know my own limits, my own state of mind, and so I just enjoy the journey. So I don't mind because the drugs don't matter, they are simply aiding me to get to a place I am willing to go."

Hearing me say this, Pan nodded. "I get, I like it. I knew the water was going to be cold, I also knew it would soothe my aching muscles, isn't that why they tell us to put ice on swellings and bruises? Except I didn't consciously think to myself, 'going in the water will numb my emotional pain and silence the noise in my head' – no, it was more of, 'I am done with this shit, done with this pain, I just want it to stop'. I don't remember thinking I wanted to end my life, no, that wasn't a thought… I just wanted to be alone, and under the water seemed like the best place at the time. And it was. It was like I had stepped into this other world, which I had if you think about it. Under the water there is a whole other world we know nothing about. It is weird, wonderful and wild, beautiful, silent and magical all at the same time. I remember the final breath I took as my head went under… and just sat there on the bottom of the edge of the lake… my eyes were closed." As she shared what it was like, she went almost trance-like, eyes closed. "It was so calming… like… I was in this bubble… floating… there was no sound… well, not really. I could hear the water moving, the faint beat of my heart and I felt … nothing. Well, not until I started to feel dizzy, lightheaded and as though I was going to fall backwards. I opened my eyes and the ice-cold water stung my eyes and made me want to take a deep inhale, so I started to move, and that's when I felt the cold water. I uncrossed my legs, don't remember doing that, but I remember them unfolding and as I stood up I had this rush of sickness and thought I was going to faint, so I just took my time and then before I knew it was walking out of the water. Like I said, I am glad I made the fire before I went in. I hadn't had much food, and the cold had made me even hungrier. I did pass out, not for long – well, not that I knew. That's when I first met Nuliajuk, she was the one who helped me get warm and stop the hyperthermia setting in."

"Yeah, not sold on that. Any of it. Cold water for a start, Desert Boy here!" said Abdu raising his hand. "Being underwater, feeling sick, fainting? You're not selling this freediving malarkey very well."

Pan laughed, "Oh, that's not freediving, that was just my first time being in the cold water and knowing I could hold my breath for a long period of time, understanding the silence and solitude I was after was under the water. Freediving is done all over the world, mainly in places such as the tiny remote islands in the Philippines, Maldives... no cold water there... well not on the surface anyway. Once you get down past about 10 metres, that's when the water starts getting cold. That's why we all wear a 3mm wetsuit, more if we freedive around here. Around here you would need about 9mm in the core of the suit and 4.5mm on the joints. In the Indian Ocean you could dive for hours. Around here though? I wouldn't dive for more than 30-50 minutes depending on the season. Making sure you get out the water and jump around fire... and not naked either." She ended with a smirk and a nod towards Abdu and me, and the reference to naked fire dancing I had made earlier.

"The bit about it being silent... that's very appealing... I could do with no disturbances a lot of the time. My head is always full of ideas, thoughts and nonstop chatter," said Abdu. "You've been a bit quiet, Babe. You okay?"

"Yeah, I'm fine," I smiled. "Just thinking and imagining being under the water. It's making me feel happy, calm, like I want to go for a swim, under the water."

"You know if she ever leaves me, it will be for the ocean," laughed Abdu.

"I got married for life Abdu, you know that," I reminded him.

"I know," he said, blowing me a kiss.

"Well, I don't know about you two, but I am really bloody hungry. I could do with a feast. I mean these supplies of Noah's eggs and sausages are alright, but remember we leave some of them for the next travellers. Who's up for heading back to the city or venturing a little further somewhere else?" asked Pan.

We chose to head back to the city via a small town, circling back rather than just turning back. As we drove, Pan shared with us more about the local area, the history and some of the flora and fauna; how most of the medicines used by the locals were all ancient remedies and the pharmacies were only kept in business by those who moved into the area, or by the doctors and nurses when things got really bad, which was hardly ever given the diet, lifestyle and mindset of the local people. They were tough people, to match the tough weather conditions and terrain, and they were grateful for life every day. The locals were the native Alaskans and their families, and those chosen by the locals to become a local – people like Pan, who was not Alaskan but had become one of them over the years. Anyone else was either a neighbour or a tourist. She also told us it was rare for someone like Nuliajuk to appear and embrace outsiders, and the fact that she had embraced me in the way she had would instantly make me one of the locals. Nuliajuk was an elder, one of the wise women of the region, and for both Pan and I to be outsiders, and yet be embraced by her would give us a standing in the community many locals would not achieve.

This made me curious and I knew my field of study into alternative medicines, therapy and healing, ancient knowledge and past lives, had taken on more importance than many of the other subjects I was studying; I knew the elusive answers to my endless questions would someday present themselves. I knew it, deep down inside of me, in a place I didn't know how to describe, where I imagined my soul lived, my very essence of being, smaller than the molecules but larger than anything I could ever imagine.

SEVEN

THE WORLD OF BOOKS

Returning home that night, I made myself a pot of tea and opened up my laptop. I was eager to read the rest of the email from Pan. Memories of our time together in Alaska had filled my mind all day. I had been slightly distracted during a couple of the meetings, but with everything going on in my life at that moment, no one said a word. They just accepted that I would be distracted. There was so much catching up to be done between Pan and I. I had children now, was a single mum, building a new business and a published author.

I had also started open water swimming, had been paying closer attention to freediving and was saving up to become a dive instructor. I knew she would be happy I had finally 'got my arse into gear' (quite literally, the dive gear) and taken the plunge; all puns intended. We had shared sporadic emails over the years and she had travelled all over the world with her diving. With each email I received I felt a large shift in her energy. Amongst news updates of Noah, Nuliajuk and what was going in in the town of

Anchorage, there was also an invitation to join her somewhere in the world and get my arse underwater with her. Some of the photos she sent were incredible, as she had also taken up underwater photography. The more emails she sent me, the more the desire to live my ocean life became stronger; on it, in it and deep beneath the surface.

Having had problems with my second pregnancy, I thought any chance of me diving was over, but she had told me in her best British accent to 'stop being so daft', of course I would be able to freedive and get my dive masters if I wanted to. In fact, the breathing practices would help restore my lung capacity. If anything could help me restore my breathing, I was more than happy to try it. She sent me a list of yoga and deep breath work practices and had laughed when I told her about my on-off love affair with yoga over the years.

Cosied up on the couch with a cuppa, and enough time to read her email before the boys finished school, I braced myself. Her emails were a joy to read, but there was always a bombshell somewhere in them.

> *So last time I sent you an email, I was telling you about this total badass Dottie Frazier, she is the one who paved the way for women like me in freediving. Basically, she pioneered women's freediving when she started teaching it back in the 1940s! Can you believe it? The 1940s! She was also the first woman in the USA to become a certified scuba instructor – which reminds me, have you got your certification yet? I bet it would have been amazing to do it in Egypt, shame about that whole uprising thing, hey?*

I loved and hated how she brushed over the Egyptian Uprising in the way she did, but I knew it was because she just couldn't get her head around stuff like that. She had never been one for politics. It reminded her too much of her uncle and the games he played to manipulate local government and funded his way into accessing other young girls through community projects.

You would love this woman! She is a real renegade in the world of both diving and women. Her dive shop was the first female owned dive shop ever, well I think so, I mean publicly known first female owned, who knows who owns half of these dive shops in the remote islands, hey? These unassuming women sat there in the shops and people will always think it is the men who own them, and I bet half of them are owned by the women. Always the way. Anyway, again, I know off tangent, but you know how you love penguins, well her dive shop is called Penguin Dive Shop so there is no excuse for you to not remember that name when you get here. You are going to come back one day, aren't you? I mean, I know I keep travelling and you have the boys, how are they by the way, are they good? Bet they are growing up to be great young men. And how's Abdu? Crazy times for you all living in Egypt.

Hey, actually, you must be back in the UK now, where are you? Oh, I hope you are, bloody scary stuff going on in Egypt, and hey, well… that comes from someone like me with a really fucking scary past. So anyway, again, I know… I bet you are smiling or laughing at me, and you can probably hear the excitement in my voice, yeah, good news this time… no bombshell… well there is one but let me just tell you this bit of news first.

You know I told you that I had always wanted to go somewhere warm and dive, go all traditional and do some freediving with the local fishermen… guess who is going to the bloody Maldives!!! YES!!! ME!!! WTAF!!! Hahaha!!! I can't believe it!!! Entered this competition in a magazine ages ago, sponsored by said amazing woman Dottie, hence why I have just gone all penguin on you gushing about this woman, and I only went and won it didn't I? Diving gear, 'all expenses trip to dive in the beautiful crystal-clear waters in the Maldives, taking in the local cuisine and local heritage, diving in some of the most exquisite locations in the world' lifted that right out of the winning email! Hahaha! And guess who else is going to be there… You are not going to believe it… only Herbert Nitsch, the world record holder for freediving… He's freediving royalty and known as the deepest man on earth! And get this…. He's gone to 214 metres! I mean who does that! But, can you imagine?

I could imagine Pan getting all excited and see her all animated, arms waving all over the place and her big ice blue eyes wide with disbelief as she was reading all about these people. If there was one thing her and I had in common, other than the ocean, it was books. The big difference between us though was she had an almost photographic memory; I was absolutely sure of it. She could tell you depths, times, milligrams of blood and oxygen units, both in the water as well as your body. She knew the different kelp and marine life in the different spots around the world and if it had anything to do with the body's respiratory system, then she could tell you all you needed to know in a heartbeat, or as she liked to say, "in a breath". She took the science, the history and the geography from around the world and looked at how she could become the best freediver she could. She analysed how performance in terms of depth and time were affected by the salt content in particular areas of the world, as well as the temperature of the water.

In one of her last emails she had told me one of the reasons why she preferred the ice-cold water was because she stayed still for longer, relying on the warmth of the dive suit rather than the water to keep her warm. She analysed the food she ate days before, weeks before and how different protein versus mineral content impacted her dive, and she always made sure she had some white chocolate on hand for immediately after a dive, with a jacket potato and vegan chilli to eat 30 minutes after coming out of the water. Her ritual before a dive consisted of drinking a minimum of two litres of turmeric and cinnamon tea as it "warms you up when you pee inside the wetsuit so you can stay down for longer". Following a dive she moved her body slowly and carefully with yoga which consisted of child's pose, warrior pose, and a few others to get the body warmed up and the blood pumping. She had tried jumping up and down afterwards but found it made her dizzier than yoga. So Pan, being Pan, started to study how the impact of extremely cold temperatures in freediving followed by sudden exercise impacted the brain. She already knew that if you didn't rise to the surface with a steady pace, then the nitrogen bubbles could rush to your brain causing brain damage – both short term and long-term depending on how long you had been diving – as well as your overall health. So jumping out of ice-cold water and then jumping around like a lunatic to warm up just didn't make sense to her at all. Plus, moving too quickly after being still in the water for so long, not only increased the risks of decompression sickness on the way up, but would probably make you pass out or throw up when you reached the surface. She had joked with me that nothing would stop her "eating jacket potato and chilli afterwards, as that's one of the highlights".

Reading the email and hearing the excitement in her words reminded me one of our calls when she told me how excited she would get reading about the worlds she would learn about in her books. Preferring to read about the world we lived in, rather than worlds of make believe where everything was all wonderful and flowery was so far removed from her own traumatic life that she just found them tedious. She much preferred learning about the real world and how Russia had sold Alaska to America for $7.2 million USD back in 1867 after the Crimean War when the Russian Tzar Alexander II had, as Pan put it "spent all his dough on killing everyone and had got bored, so needed more money to create another war with another country". She did find it amusing how not long after "the Russian dude" had lost out BIG TIME when all the Russians left, and the gold rush began in 1896. "Shot himself in the foot there, didn't he!"

I smiled at this memory because in some ways I was grateful she would hide away in her room night after night to avoid being around anyone when she was younger. Her trauma had led her to knowledge and taken her away from having to "go down to dinner" for polite conversation with the monster and his friends who would brag about the success in their day, whilst her mum and her sat there knowing who he really was. The things Pan knew about so many subjects was incredible. Her book recommendations were textbooks, factual books, memoirs, biographies, and like me, she would be able to devour a book in no time at all, with a recall like no one else I had ever known.

Going back to her email I realised I still had about an hour before the boys needed picking up from school and depending on what the bombshell was that she had promised me further down the email, I could always call the school and ask them to put the boys in after school clubs, something they had both been asking me about.

So, anyway… God how many times am I going to use that word in this email? So, yeah! I've won this crazy prize and I am leaving in a few days! I can't quite believe it and I just had to write and tell you, because I know you will get it. Like how many times have we spoken about swimming in hot tropical waters together because you are too chicken to come and dive with me here in Alaska. I will get you here you know, and YOU WILL come diving with me one day. What is really funny though, not haha funny, but interesting funny, is cryostasis. I've been studying it to help me improve my dive times here in the cold north. You know I am a geek, and you know I love studying just as much as you, well almost I think, probably more, who knows, who cares, but cryostasis. Mental as you like. Basically, not to go too nerdy on you, but you know when I was telling you about how I only feel the cold when I move in the ice water, well, I reckon – and you know, I am still only learning about this shit, but when I am in the icy water and I switch off, remember I told you it feels like I have gone to sleep? Well apparently this cryostasis is, wait for it 'suspended animation like a deep sleep at super low temperatures' so I reckon, that I am reversing the ageing process with this whole freediving in icy water. Makes sense right? Well to me it does, and no wonder I am so youthful looking! Haha! All joking aside, I do wonder about all the affects this is having on my body. I know I love it down there and I know it is my happy place, but really what am I doing?

Reading this last sentence I knew she was about to share with me the bombshell she had referred to earlier in her email. I knew it had something to do with her health and I was not sure I wanted to read this before the boys came home from school, because if it was something really bad, I didn't want to be upset in front of them. I finished my tea and closed my laptop. Put on my boots, called my dog and we made our way to the car. I couldn't stop tapping my fingers on the steering wheel as I drove, feeling impatient and wanting to know what she had written; and then I remembered she had started the email with saying she was going to answer the question I had left her with, the one where I had asked her about staying quiet, knowing what she knew, and how'd she'd feel if she found out he had done it to another young girl. The look on her face when I asked her was one of pain, anger, confusion and fear. She had been majorly pissed off with me and I had hoped it hadn't killed off our short friendship before it had even started.

When I arrived back in the UK, there was a postcard waiting for me with the words:

I want to tell you to fuck off, but I know you are right. Leave it with me. I love you and I hate you all at the same time,

love Pan xx

I still had that postcard. It captured the cabin and the forest where we had stayed the 'night of the deep dive', the name we gave to our journey together with Nuliajuk.

My thoughts then passed to Nuliajuk. Was it her? Was she sick? Had she passed over? Probably not, she would probably outlive us all. She defied the aging process and she had never been anywhere near the state of cryostasis!

Before I knew it, I was at the school and I just didn't want to go in and be social with the other parents, not today, but I had to go in and collect my youngest, knowing my eldest would make his way over to the prep school by himself. No sooner had I put my dog on the lead and crossed the road, I saw my eldest coming along by the botanical gardens. I let the lead go and watched my son and fur baby embrace each other, hearing excitement from both of them, knowing they were safe, I walked down to the school. As soon as I got to the gate, my youngest spotted me and ran to me. "Hiya Mummy, how was your day?" Always the same, always the first words he spoke. He made my heart burst with love and then joy as he asked, "What's for dinner?"

We discussed what we would make when we got home as we walked back to the car, meeting his brother and our dog on the way. It was in these moments when the four of us were together that my happiest memories were made, and I knew that whatever happened, I would always have them.

Arriving home, the boys headed to the park with our dog. I told them I had received a friend's email and I really wanted to read it but would read it later because it was a really long one, and we had things to do, like homework and dinner to cook. I also told them there was possibly some sad news in it. My eldest in all his wisdom told me, "Well you had better read it before we go to bed so we can hug you if you need one." So that was that – decided upon. They would go to the park, I'd read the rest of the email and then we would eat, do homework and snuggle on the couch, regardless of the outcome of the email.

Putting the kettle on, waiting for it to boil, I prepped the jacket potatoes and smiled because it had been the boys who had suggested we have jacket potatoes and chilli in honour of my friend. Giving them just enough detail about her to help them to connect with her seemed like a good idea, and as the potatoes went into the oven, coated in olive oil, sea salt and cracked black pepper, I smiled to myself. They'd like her, she'd like them. One day we would hopefully be all together on a beach somewhere, somewhere cold, like Alaska. Ideas were forming in the recesses of my mind, and then the kettle was boiled, water poured over the tea bag and I went into the lounge to resume the position on the couch, with my cream chunky fisherman socks on. Essential night-time attire in a less than tropical location, even if only in a vest top and shorts to sleep in.

Laptop open, tea at the ready, I opened the email again and started reading.

Like seriously, what am I doing to my body? All this pressure going to my organs, all this nitrogen in my blood and rushing to my brain, and I have to wonder if I have actually dealt with any of the pain and trauma from all those years ago, or if I have just been avoiding it by numbing the pain with this cold-water therapy. I mean, I know I have healed loads Moana, but seriously sometimes when I come out of a deep dive in the coldest of water, and I am sat in my little place, by the fire in my warm chunky fisherman socks and jumper, all alone, I have to wonder if I have healed.

I smiled at the fact that I was wearing a pair of the chunky knit fisherman socks, and when I looked at them, they were actually the pair she had sent me years ago, still going strong; unlike the pair of us by the sound of things.

If I had truly healed myself, don't you think I would have had a life partner, been able to trust someone with my body and with my heart instead of running, or rather diving headfirst into the abyss? Mum found love with Dad. You found love, and so do others, and I know we are all different but, sometimes I wonder why I am still all alone and why I keep doing this. I know I am getting older now, but I would love to have someone to go to the Maldives with, and maybe that is it, the prize was for me and a partner, and I don't have one. I would love to take you, but you have Abdu and the boys, and if I remember you have a dog now too. SO cute by the way! And who do I have? No one. Mum and Dad died years ago, and I have no one, and it fucking sucks at times. Mostly I like it, I wouldn't say I love it, but I like it. I don't get to compromise on what to eat, where to go, or how to decorate my cabin or which truck to buy, but I think I would like to. I have hidden myself away in books and research, in my diving and built a big 'fuck off!' wall around my heart, like literally I am sure that is what every bloody brick I have used to build that wall says on it, and I work hard, study harder and dive deeper just so I don't have to think about a partner or feel anything. There is no space in my life for someone else, and what if, what if I need someone to take care of me? I know that seems selfish, but it's not just about that is it? It's about having that person to giggle with, get excited with, make plans with and travel the world together with. It's too late for me to have children, but I don't want to also die knowing that he robbed me of love as well as everything else he robbed me of.

I could tell as I read these words she was crying, and the anger and the deep sadness had returned. I wondered if she had lost a friend whilst diving, or seen a friend suffer from the delayed painful ill effects of the bends. Had she been attracted to someone but not allowed herself to love another? There were so many questions running through my mind, and as I was just about to return to the email, I felt a tear fall roll down my face. Here we both were approaching our forties and although happy with our lives in general, and really intelligent, beautiful women, both alone and with a wall of ice around our hearts, for very different reasons. She would be sad to know that Abdu and I had divorced, but happy to know we were still friends. Well, as good a friend as you can be with someone who lies and betrays you for almost twenty years. I understood the trust issues she was having, hers with herself and me with others. How could I really truly trust my instincts if I had been fooled by them for so long? How could she trust a relationship with someone when most people these days only wanted sex. She didn't want sex. She wanted love and all her life she had never had it. Her mother and father loved her, but she blocked her father's love believing he was controlling her mother, and that he must have known what her uncle was up to. Nuliajuk loved her but was always the magically appearing and disappearing healer. Noah loved her like his own daughter, but Pan didn't know how to receive a hug, and like she had said to me many times, "How can you accept love when you can't even accept a hug? How can you be intimate with a guy, when you cannot even be alone in a room with a guy?"

She had filled her life with research for her marine biology masters, researching the marine life around Alaska, and combining that with her fascination of the fact that as freedivers they were more likely to have the mammalian diving reflex, something which only aquatic mammals such as seals, dolphins and otters had. The more she learnt about it, the more she believed this meant we could actually be originally from the ocean, and if we were from the ocean, what was the connection to Atlantis? She fully believed that Atlantis was a place and had argued many times that the Atlantic was the key to the discovery of it "because they are a bit too close in name for it to be a coincidence". She didn't need to convince me, and we had spent many hours researching new data and sharing videos and book titles on different theories of Atlantis.

I know you are reading this thinking about all the things which could have happened with friends who are divers, and I know you know I am crying now… even after the excitement of my HUGE prize, but that is how I am at the moment. A fellow female freediver joked with me that I have the menopause coming on, and it is not something that I had considered to be honest with you. Why would I? I have had no one to teach me or guide me or let me know it is coming. I mean, it is not like I sit here and ask myself when my body is going to send me into manic hormonal depression and take away my opportunity to have children. And you know, I think that maybe I would have wanted to have them, now that I know I can't, well suspect that I can't. It's one thing knowing you can choose not to have something but once that choice is taken away, you suddenly want something you have never wanted, or at least didn't think you wanted. Can you tell my head is a shed at the moment? A messy, disorganised, shed where Noah keeps everything from his chicken troughs to his hooving knives. He's a good man, such a sweetheart, and I know he is the closest person I have ever allowed in my life to be family. Notice I own it now, the allowing people to be in my life, but this whole allowing love in your life, not as easy for people like me.
So I will tell you, a friend of mine, a guy friend, one who I thought a lot of, well he made a pass at me a few weeks back. Apparently he has liked me for ages, and well we were talking on the beach after we had all been diving for the

weekend. It was great, there must have been about 12 of us. Fires were burning, food was cooking, coffee was brewing, music playing and many of us were singing and dancing. A weekend out under the stars and it was blissful. One of those long weekends… what was it you and Abdu call them? Bank Holiday Benders, or at least you did do 'back in the day'. You two are so funny. Well, there we were sitting chatting, discussing the reflex bradycardia – that's a drop in heart rate to you, and how vasoconstriction (narrowing of the blood vessels) and splenic contraction impact the body when we are diving deep into the icy water, but are at high altitude, so the body gets confused, because even when out of the water, the air pressure is lighter and so not only do we have altitude sickness to deal with but also decompression sickness. So you can see, we were having a really in-depth conversation and the way in which he was using the actual words for the different terms was making me all excited and I felt my pussy go all warm and I really wanted to kiss him and… fuck!… not as in fuck I wanted to fuck him, although… but fuck as in here I am almost in my forties and I have finally got to the point where I want to kiss a man. I have never done that before Moana. I have never allowed myself to be with a man. HE was the last man to even touch me and then I started freaking out that I don't want him to be the only man to have been inside me, and then freaked out that I have left it this long and now I don't know what to do and this friend is so fucking intelligent he makes me want to kiss him and do all kinds of things to him. Is this what it feels like? To have the hots for someone, because I am telling you, it gets pretty damn hot down there when I think about him, and if so how do you actually be with someone? I wish you were here… I know you would know… and you should hear him say words like latent hypoxia and hypoxic blackout instead of just 'blackouts'. He is so intelligent, but also wise you know. When he hears someone criticise us for being reckless with our lives, for putting ourselves in danger, he doesn't dismiss them, he invites them so kindly to have a conversation with him, shares information about the lung function and how body awareness is improved and how much more we are aware of breathing and water safety. Watching him with others and the way he so patiently explains everything, oh Moana! And then what did I do? Yep, fucked it up. He was sat there with me all night, and I thought he was going to make a move and I just got up and said I needed to get another drink, and he looked sad and confused, and all I wanted to do was kiss him. And now I am telling you all this I feel like a stupid 12-year-old asking her friend to find out what to do with the hunky boy at the back of the class. Oh why are you not here?

I was smiling and crying all at the same time, relieved that she had now allowed herself to feel something, and I knew that once I had read the entire email and had time to respond to her in full, I would make sure she understood that the fact she *could* feel something now meant that she had healed so much of what that monster had broken inside of her. She had done so much work on herself. She'd had another couple of journeys with Nuliajuk, had her womb cleansed through energy work, done cord cutting meditations and all the other magical stuff she had been told about. But each and every time she got like this, I knew she would resort to going walkabout on a Mick Dundee style 'out bush' transcendence walk. She would be gone for another week at least, and that was just the walking, it didn't include the days on end she would dive until she couldn't dive anymore due to the physical exhaustion. Then the reality hit me. She had sent this email to me today, this morning… Alaska was nine hours behind me… so if she had sent it to me before lunch my time… that meant she had either stayed up really late unable to sleep, or she had been tossing and turning all night unable to sleep. I looked at the clock on the wall. It was just gone 5 pm, so it would be 8 am… too early to call if she had stayed awake late, or had been tossing and turning all night, but I had to call her. I didn't want her going diving in this headspace, or walkabout for that matter. Then I remembered what she had once said to me: "When you enter the water in pain or fear, she will intensify it, and not open up to you, but when you enter her with calmness in your heart, then the experience is pure magic".

Remembering this brought a sense of relief because I knew no matter how bad things were, there would be no way she would go diving. She had too much respect for the water, especially the ocean, these days. The memory also brought back the giggles I'd had back then thinking about how it was a great metaphor for a man entering a woman. I found myself rubbing my left shoulder where she had slapped me for having such a 'one track mind'. She was right though, the ocean presents to you what is already within you. She responds back with what you give her; if you let go and surrender to her, the dance between you will be harmonious like a dance of love. I made up my mind in that moment the boys and I would head to the beach that weekend for a road trip.

Knowing and trusting Pan wouldn't do something stupid, I settled back to the email, especially given she may have changed her energy by the end of the email, and just by writing what she had written, she would more than likely feel better given I had shown her how to 'purge it all out'.

EIGHT

NUMBING THE PAIN

There's another reason I wish you were here, or at least closer, and when I tell you, you are going to understand why I need you, no, sorry, want you here. Fuck it! No, I needed you here, but I did get through it, so I guess I didn't need you here… aahhhh! See what you do with your precision of words and perspectives. Sometimes I wish you would keep them to yourself! They are so bloody annoying, especially when I want to wallow in self-pity but your words ringing around in my head won't let me.

Now I had read this last bit of the email I was glad I hadn't jumped on the phone and called her. I could tell instantly that she was getting back to the determined Pan I had grown to love so deeply over the years.

So, I am now going to answer that question you asked me way back then. So you know how much I have changed over the years, and even had my nose done and sorted out my mouth after the beating the monster himself gave me? Well, I needed a new set of fins and the only place I could get them was in Vancouver. They are so cool by the way, slightly weighted so I don't have to have as many weights around my waist and stops me moving my body as much in the water when descending, and we both know I don't like moving much in cold water because I feel the cold so much. It also means I can go deeper and stay for longer in my happy place. It took me ages to psyche myself up just to go into Vancouver, let alone go downtown, but I thought I had changed more than enough for no one to recognise me. Oh how wrong I was, and of all bloody places to be recognised, I was in the main collections depot at Canada Post in Woodland Dr, not that it would mean anything to you, but you will love the number of the address… 333. Yep! You read that right, 3 bloody 33! Can you believe it? So I once I got out of my head, I knew it had to mean something right? I really do think I am turning into you at times with your bloody angel numbers, but being all geek about it, I went down the numerology route of study for a while. Fascinating subject, yes, like you said it would be and yes I can hear you giggling to yourself as you read this. Bitch. Hahaha! We make me laugh. I bloody love you. Anyway, as I was saying, there I was thinking I was all incognito and the woman behind the glass screen just kept looking at me. I got majorly paranoid as if I had just smoked a tonne of weed, and wanted to run out of the place, but I held it together, you would be so proud of me by the way. I had filled in the little postcard thing and handed over my ID and her face went white. No word of a fucking lie. White I tell you! And that is coming from me, old ghost carp over here, or 'Ghostie' as some of the dive gang have taken to calling me. I thought it was going to be me who had the wobble, but it was her! Her hands started shaking and I saw this rush of emotions in her face and tears prick her eyes, and the next thing I know, she is gone. With my address postcard proof of delivery thing and my ID. It took me a good 20-30 seconds to call out after her, but just as I was opening my mouth, this other woman comes in and handles the parcel for me. Leaving the depot, I just wanted to get out of there, but I needed a coffee and there was a coffee shop just around the corner. I was now shaking wondering what the hell all that meant, and nearly ended up knocking over a display stand of bags of coffee beans… can you imagine those going everywhere? I finally order my coffee, wait at the end of the counter for it to arrive and all of a sudden she's there! YEP! After running out on me, she comes up to me as meek and mild something or other, and she asks, "Is it really you Pandora?"

Hearing that name, I felt my legs go weaker than having the bends on a bad dive. "Sorry do I know you?" were the first words that came out of my mouth, and I felt cruel and relieved all at the same time. Relieved that I hadn't said, "Who the fuck are you?" And cruel because for her to have reacted in the way she did when she saw my name, and to now come up to me, that took some guts. I knew why she had reacted the way she did, I knew he had done it to her too. Don't ask me how I knew, but I knew. And that is why I am ready to answer your question. It felt awful, like I had allowed it to happen. Like I had knowingly given him permission to do all those awful things to more people, and I could have prevented it. I know I was still processing my own journey; I know it is not my fault, but seeing her face, hearing that name, it all came crashing down on me and I wanted to run and find the nearest ice-cold lake I could. But how could I when she had shown such courage?

"You don't have a reason to know me, but I knew of you. You were older than me, and I saw you around," she said before dropping her eyes and adding in an almost whisper, "And you were the one he talked about all the time." The room started spinning and I knew I was going to faint if I didn't get out of there, and that's when I heard the woman call my name to let me know my coffee was ready. I put the fins under my right arm, grabbed my coffee, and grabbed this poor young girl with my left hand, almost dragging her out of the coffee shop, across the road to where I had parked my truck. I told her to get in Moana, almost shouted it at her, and as she did, I threw my beautiful new fins I hadn't even had time to look at in the back seat, jumped in the front, and started driving. I had no idea where we were going and she knew it. She told me to take her to her apartment where we could talk, because she 'needed' to talk with me. And you know what? I felt that. Deep in my core, I felt her need to talk, like I had done all those years, so I drove to this address in this daze of emotional confusion. We'd arrived before I knew it and I had never been to this part of town before, and as I was about to get out of the truck I realised I couldn't feel anything. It was like I was having an episode of the bends on dry land, playing with the edges of dizziness and drowning, strength and weakness and just like when I am under water and I feel these sensations, it gave me a rush. I got a fucking rush on the intensity of the dizziness, and you know what? It made me more determined to be there for her, to be stronger for myself to see this through, just like I do when I want to push for a personal best in the water, going for longer, going deeper, *both drowning out noise from above… and what started as a need to numb my pain and block out the sounds of his voice, became a passion of mine, a sport I love and then I heard him laughing at me. Can you fucking believe that? I heard him laughing at me as though he was so arrogant he knew he had given me this gift of freediving because without the terror he gave me I would never have gone to the lake, would never have walked into the ice-cold water, never discovered my talent for holding my breath for so long; I would not have my passion for the ocean, wouldn't have studied the environment and marine life and wouldn't have hidden away in the books so much. I hated him so much more in that moment, that I actually wanted to stab him, kill him and yet also in that moment this calm came over me like never before. I had experienced something similar in the water, in those moments of almost panic, but this, this was next level, and I knew Moana, I knew I wanted to stop him. I wanted to see him suffer, to see him lose everything, but more importantly, I wanted to protect others, I wanted to stop him and his kind; I wanted to let all those who had suffered from this kind of abuse that there was a wonderful life they could create for themselves in spite of them, not because of them, but because of THE POWER WITHIN THEM.*

Tears were rolling down my face at this point and I couldn't help feeling so proud of her for what she had now declared for herself, and that she had finally got to the point where she was no longer afraid of facing him in the courtroom, of facing him and taking away his power, because no matter what happened from this point on, now she had declared that for herself, within herself, she was going to be so much more unstoppable in every area of life. I looked at the clock again and realised it was almost time to take the potatoes out of the oven and go get the boys from the park. But as I started to close the laptop, the front door opened, and our dog came running in and jumped up on the couch next to me. "Hello handsome, how was the park, hey? Are you ready for your dinner?"

"We're back!" Came the voices of my boys in unison, along with the words, "Ah, they smell good!"

My youngest declared he was grating the cheese, only to have my oldest declare he wanted to and then the bickering began and the accusations of "you just want to eat the cheese as you grate it" started and the laughing of them knowing the reason they both wanted to grate the cheese was because they both wanted to eat the cheese. The eldest came up with the solution, "You make Mum's tea, because she likes yours better than mine, and I will cut us both a chunk of cheese to eat, and will I grate the rest of it." The deal was sealed, the tea was being made, the cheese was being grated, with me taking the jacket potatoes out to check on them. With my tea made, my youngest made our dog his dinner and then said, "Hey! You tricked me! Mum likes your tea better than mine! You just knew you didn't have to feed Shadow!" These boys!

"So how's your friend? Have you finished her email yet?" asked my eldest.

"Not quite finished it, but she's good. In fact, she has had a really powerful breakthrough, and she's won a freediving holiday in the Maldives!" I answered.

"Where's that?" my youngest asked.

"In the Indian Ocean near Madagascar," answered my eldest to my surprise.

"What, with the penguins and Alex the Lion and Gloria? Yeah! Let's watch that tonight whilst we have dinner! We haven't watched that for ages!"

"After dinner and the washing up, and you have a deal," I said.

"Done!" both boys said together.

And so with that we finished making and eating dinner, enjoying a night snuggled up on the couch together.

NINE

FROZEN IN THE MOMENT

Bedtime stories read, snuggles and laughter had, the boys were now fast asleep. Oh, how I loved watching them sleep. Their little faces, the sound of their breathing, there was nothing in the world I loved more than lying next to them watching them sleep. They were my world, my reason for getting up in the morning, and I had to be brave and strong for them.

Abdu had gone to America to be with his fiancé and not been in contact with them for months. Keeping the boys happy, focused on their schoolwork and providing for them were my main objectives at this moment in time, and so far I was getting there, day-by-day I was breaking through the pain barrier, so it was no surprise to me that Pan would now also be going through something similar in her life. Our lives were so different, and the things we passed through, emotionally and mentally, presented us with challenges so alike that we were always there to support each other from a place of understanding, rather than the 'empty understanding' others offered in moments of perceived crisis.

Since my divorce, I had seen the truth of friendships I'd had for years. It had been a wakeup call like no other, and I was glad I had seen them for what they were.

Heading downstairs I knew I had work to do on my business, but I had to finish the email. I had to know whether my friend needed me or not, especially given the breakthrough she had just had. I put the kettle on for a cuppa, and then realised a certain fur baby wanted to go for a walk, so I put my boots and coat on and went out into the night air. It was just what I needed, and I knew that once I had finished reading the email, I would need another walk before bed. Walking around the local area, in the silence of the night, I was so glad we had nothing but the peak district national parks as our back garden. The night sky was lit up with stars and the silence was wonderful. Pan would have loved it. The only problem I had with it though was that it was so far away from the ocean. That said it did give the three of us and Shadow the opportunity to go on road trips to the coast on any given weekend. Walking around the corner of the last block, I had a sudden chill, 'as if someone had passed over my grave' as my nan would say. I didn't like it when that happened and so I called Shadow, who came bounding up the road in all his cuteness. This dog, if he was a man… he'd be the perfect partner.

Back in the house, the kettle went back on, and we got ourselves ready for the rest of the email. Shadow was already on the couch by the laptop ready when I walked in the lounge in my chunky socks, carrying my tea. "Ready then, boy? The final instalment. Let's find out what she's been up to shall we?"

I won't go into the details of everything she told me, you already know what he did to me, and let's just say a leopard doesn't change his spots, except this time he taunted her with his memories of me and my mum. That poor girl heard it all, and she told me things he had done to my mum, thinking he had taunted me with those stories too. She was a mess, and the tears and hugs we shared that night. Moana, he is one evil sick bastard, and by the end of the night we had already decided we were going to join forces and go to the police. We had to. Neither of us were willing to allow this to happen to someone else. Why should another go through what we went through at his hands, at any monsters hands? I know now that when we remain silent, we give them permission, and that by staying silent we allow others to suffer. We have already been through the worst of it, the memories are just memories and they will haunt us so long as we run from them. So stand up and fight back is the only way to transform these memories, like I have transformed the ice-cold water as a way to numb the pain, into the way in which I get to see the beauty of a different kind of underworld. I numbed my pain to numb the memories, to hide from the world and silence his voice, but by doing that I silenced my own voice. I get it now, and I know it took me long enough to get it, but I got it, and all because I ordered some sexy ass new dive fins. They really are beautiful fins Mo, something only a diver would understand I know, but the first time I wore them, I felt the power of that conversation with this young girl, and I smashed all my personal bests in diving – how's that for a release of the past, hey? The words out of my mouth when the adjudicator told me my time and depth were no other than "FUCK YEAH!" – it was all the motivation I needed to take the next step of writing it all out in a journal. Every memory I had, every time it happened, every sick motherfucking thing that monster did to me, and I made copies. There was no way I was going to send it to some lawyer and then have them bury it because they turned out to be on his payroll. I copied it dozens of times so it couldn't be buried. I sent copies to all the Vancouver State and Canadian national newspapers, radio stations, to three different law firms. I even sent a copy to the marketing department of the 'family business' and told them to 'put a spin on this shit' letting them know which newspapers and radio stations had it, not telling them which law firms had it, and I sent copies to the heads of department in the Sex Crimes Unit at the Vancouver State Police Department. I sent copies to the BC Women's Organisation which deals with sexual abuse, because my thinking was if he had done it to the three of us, who else had he done it to. I never heard back from two of the law firms, and a couple of the media channels wouldn't touch it until it was proven, and of course I never heard from the firm, but I did hear from his lawyers. I burnt that letter and sent the ashes back in an envelope to them, telling them I would see him in court. Moana, I felt so powerful in all of those moments and then when I heard back from the lawyers saying they could not get involved, and the police said there was not enough evidence to convict him, I didn't know what to do. So I did the only think I know how to do, I went diving again. I knew the answers would come to me on a dive, I just knew it, so I chose my favourite dive spot, and you are going to love this name… Resurrection Bay… what better name for a dive when you want to come back fighting right? Yeah, I can see you smiling, and I bet you have had at least four cups of tea whilst reading this bloody novel of an email! Haha! It's alright, I will tell you, tell the world my story, because I sure as hell wouldn't be able to tell it the way you can. How would that be, hey? You and me, rising up together again and nailing this bastard together… yeah that would be ace. Do it! And if I ever change my mind, ignore me. Seriously, because it would only be self-doubt and fear which holds us all prisoner and serves no one. We've got to do this, and I know you are the person to do it. I trust you Mo, I really trust you, and I know you know that. Maybe after all this is done, and the bastard has gone down for it, you can then write the book, but it may be too late then, but you will know when the time is right.

Reading this last part of the email, my heart was racing, and I was so proud of her and the action she had taken. Bloody loved the name of the lake she was going to go and resurrect her power too. I also did a quick count of how many cups of tea I'd had since I'd started reading the email and it was four! I couldn't believe it! "She's right Shadow, I have had four cups of tea! She knows me so well, doesn't she my lovely." I took a break from reading and had cuddles with him, had a game of tug of war and chased him around the lounge. "I am sorry I haven't given you much attention today my angel, tomorrow we will go on one of our long walks. You'll like that I know you will. Be good to walk off a few of these emotions to be honest with you. Where do you want to go? Mayfield or Lady Cannington's? Or how about both? Shall we have a look at Mummy's calendar?" Having had a look at the calendar, it would have to be Lady Cannington's because I knew if we started on the Mayfield Valley walk I wouldn't be back in time to get everything done I wanted to get done before the boys needed picking up from school. "Right then mister, let's finish this email shall we? Then another walk and then bed." Within seconds he was back up on the couch next to the laptop ready to snuggle up as I read the final parts of the email. "You're a good boy aren't you," I said giving him a kiss on the forehead, and a tickle behind the ears, which he gave me a kiss on the hand in return. "I do love you fluffy butt, so much."

I arrived at Resurrection Bay and it was a perfect day for diving. The air wasn't cold, well to you it would be, but for me, the conditions were perfect. There had been no wind or rainstorms which meant the water would be as clear as crystal, and the temperature of the water was perfect at what you Brits call 16 degrees celsius. I planned on being up there for a week, that way I could not just dive for clarity but also because the orca and humpbacks would be there. Seriously, for someone who loves diving and studies marine biology and ecology, this place is amazing. I also thought I would do some study up there whilst I was at it. Well if you are going to go, might as well make the most of every minute, right? From the moment I arrived, the seals, otters and sea lions were all out playing. By day two I had seen a load of puffins and the flora under the water was just stunning. Mo, the colours of the plants, the fish, the stones and the way it is all naturally laid out. Honestly, if I could just live underwater the whole time, I would choose this place. No questions asked.

I already knew by the time I arrived at the lake that I would keep pushing for him to be exposed, but how would I do that without outing myself? You know me, I hate the attention; I didn't want my dive team knowing who I was, or what had happened. I like my life as Pan, the freediver who lives in a quiet little cottage, studying her plants. I don't want to be a member of that family; the spoilt little rich kid who 'obviously lives on a trust fund'. No, I didn't want that, and I didn't want for people who knew me in Anchorage to know I was one of the enemy either. I wasn't, I was part of Noah's tribe, I was one of him, one of Hunter, one of the locals, not one of those who were raping the lands and the oceans destroying communities and habitats in the process. I thought about the anonymous movement, I thought about hiding behind a mask, but then I wouldn't be any better than him, hiding behind this mask of a great guy, the one who the nation looked up to. The one men wanted to be like, the man women wanted to be seen with and showered with diamonds and dresses from his wallet.

On the third morning when I was preparing for my dive, I was doing my breath work and yoga, centring myself, stepping into my serenity space and BOOM, fucking BOOM! I had the idea of finding out which journalists had covered high profile sexual abuse and rape cases, which lawyers had defended the impossible cases, which smaller organisations in the Vancouver area dealt with women and girls in this kind of situation, and I started writing a letter, an anonymous tip off, including the fact that certain law firms and heads of police departments had ignored my previous letter and copies. I put my marine life and 'rabbit hole researcher' head on and man was the list a long one. Needless to say I didn't dive that day, but the yoga was good. I did dive all the next day though, not all at once, that would be stupid, and ate so many bloody nuts and fruits I might as well become bloody vegan! Still, I had clarity in mind, and bowels… apricots are great aren't they! Haha!

I tell you this though, after that day of research, my next two days of diving we some of the clearest, most focused dives I have ever done. I was on autopilot, in total flow state, you could say I had entered another dimension, another realm of existence and it was beautiful. Oh Mo, it was so beautiful. I can even feel the emotions coming up now remembering the vibrant red plants, the fern-like ones, the feathery one, all just dancing around in the water, best kind of ballet there is.

Getting back to Anchorage took me about two weeks. It's one thing to sail across the Gulf of Alaska from Vancouver to Resurrection Bay, but to get to Anchorage is a bit of a faff. Still, the Kenai Fjords looked amazing as we sailed south, and as we came up the other side of Kachemak Bay, we stopped off at Homer for some more provisions, and quite appropriate don't you think for the epic adventure that was about to unfold. I knew you will appreciate the gesture once you found out, and I can see you sat there smiling, probably sharing with Shadow that I was at Homer and telling him it was the Greek Homer not the dribbling yellow fool most people know about. How is the little fluff ball anyway? Still as cute as always? If you are back in the UK, I am guessing his nose has had a bit of an awakening after the smells of Cairo. He's probably relieved — haha! I know I would be.

Man, all those people, they gotta stink up the place… it's bad enough going into Vancouver by boat from Anchorage, and Vancouver isn't half as many people as Cairo! Or as hot, and that has got to add a whole new dynamic to the smell. Yeah, give me Anchorage any day of the week. Speaking of weeks, the weeks that followed were filled with emails going back and forth, phone calls and requests to go back to Vancouver, but I said I wanted to do everything from where I was, so there I was in Bethel with dodgy internet on the best days, trying to have a Skype call with these lawyers, journos and organisations causing a massive storm back in Vancouver, and although I wasn't there to watch it all unfold, I felt the joy of knowing I had done something to stop him doing it to another. You were right about so many things, and I know you are not the 'I told you so' kind of person but everything you have told me would work, everything you have told me to harness, the whole turning negatives into positives, the journaling, turning the 'it happened for me, not to me' (the hardest fucking pill of all to swallow I tell you!), everything you have ever invited me to dive deeper into, everything you have confronted me with, when at times I have wanted to punch you in the face, yeah… there were many of those in the early days, not that I would, but you know what I mean, they were all beautiful gifts of self-discovery and awareness, of my own personal power, and if there is one thing I am truly grateful for in my life, it's you, not that you are a thing or anything, but you know what I mean. I love you. I do you know, I really fucking love you.

"Oh Shadow!" I wept, tears falling down my face, in awe of my friend for the power she had harnessed in taking the next steps on her journey of healing, and for the courage she had taken in bringing down the monster who had stolen so much of her life, including her relationship with her mother and father, the ability to make friends, and the willingness to allow a man in her life to love her. I was proud of her for using all the skills she had learnt in her research and absorbing knowledge, of being willing to follow the links, of going to the places in her heart, mind and soul that so many would run from. I was overwhelmed by the praise she had bestowed upon me and the love she sent me through her words, and I was crying so much Shadow pushed his way onto my lap and started licking the tears off my chin, making me giggle in amongst all of it. "I think it is time for our last walk of the night don't you, boy?" Before I could close the laptop, he had already jumped down and was sat waiting for me in the doorway, looking back at me to tell me he would wait for me before he moved to the boot room at the back of the house. "I'm coming boy, go get your lead." And with that he ran off into the boot room and by the time I got there, he was sat waiting with his lead in his mouth. "You are just the cutest you know that," I said to him, with him responding with a tilt of his head to the side. "Come on then, let's go," and out the back door we went, him still carrying his own lead and the tears in my eyes being masked by the tears caused by the cold wind as they came over the moors. I loved this time of year, still cold at night, almost into summer, but not quite, and with the home I had created with the boys being so close to the moors, high up over the city, the night air always had a sharpness to it. Pan would have loved it here in winter.

I read the rest of her email as I was tucked up in bed and it finished off with her being proud of herself and excited about her up and coming prize winning trip to the Maldives with the freediving royalty. I knew she would have a really great time, she deserved to. She had been through more than enough in her lifetime, so it was about time she had her life turn around. I did smile to myself that her 'luck' had changed the moment she had taken the plunge and faced the past in such an honourable way. A new man who I hoped would stand by her side and understand there were just some things he would never know about her, but would simply accept her for who she was, and someone who would not give up at the first hurdle. Whoever he was, he would have to be someone special for her to open up herself to him, to even allow him to hug her, let alone be alone in a room with her and make love to her. I went to sleep with a smile on my face and a happy heart that she had got to the place of being like an excited teenager in love. It may be too late for her to have children, but she got to live an incredible life so many only dream of. She got to see things that many people only see in magazines, and she knew more about the planet we live on than anyone else I knew. She knew the darkness above the surface which resided in humans, and the beauty of the natural world above and below the surface. Her life was so rich in so many ways and now she had 'brought down the house' – she had also been awarded compensation which paid off her student loans, her cottage and her truck loan. The rest she gave away, millions of it, to women and children who suffer from abuse, and she set up a fund for men wrongfully accused of rape and abuse who'd had their lives shattered and destroyed by the media frenzy.

Her mother and father's original will came to the surface as well and her outstanding monthly allowance that had been set up from the company was paid to her in full, with the rest due to come every month which followed. She didn't want the money, so she split that payment between a local hospital and school in Anchorage and rehab centre in Bethel, all anonymous of course. She didn't want any of the dirty money, as she called it. She was fine being Pan, the woman who lives in the cottage over yonder who freedives and studies the world under water, and that's one of the reasons I loved her so much. She was my friend. A beautiful woman inside and out, a fellow mermaid and friend from Atlantis.

TEN

INTO THE BLUE

I looked at the date in the bottom right-hand corner of my laptop, did a quick calculation, she'd be landing in the Maldives any moment. Knowing Pan she had packed nothing but dive gear and a couple of thick jumpers as well as bikinis, maybe a sarong and that would be about it. "If it fits in more than one bag and my dive bag, it's too much." And by bag, she meant a rucksack that most kids would take to school with them. I loved how she had no attachment to material items in life, was really selective in who she surrounded herself with and was focused more on experiences rather than things. She understood the true beauty of life, and what was important. But then again, most people who had been through hell knew the real value of life.

Thinking back to the email I had sent in response to her email, I knew she would have been the mirror of me, crying, smiling and giggling, but instead of tea, she would have been drinking one of her 'sea smoothies', a combination of kelp, ginger, turmeric, apples and whatever else she had to hand. Knowing she would be making her way through a plate of waffles, reindeer sausages and eggs from Noah's backyard brought a smile to my face, and I made the choice in that moment that the boys and I would have a Pan Dinner that night. I still had some gluten free, free range, organic, halal lamb and mint sausages in the freezer, and instead of waffles, I would make American Style gluten free pancakes, with free range organic fried eggs. She would laugh at me for all these labels and tell me that I just needed to live somewhere remote and live off the grid, and I was counting down the days until that happened. Living off grid, and then just making a trip somewhere to upload my work before disappearing again… sounded perfect to me. Only a handful of people would know my whereabouts, my boys, my parents, my love and key members of my team. I just needed to build my team and I knew the love would show up in the future, when the time was right, and as my mum said, when I was least expecting it.

I wondered if the guy who Pan had run away from that night had stuck around and gone back to her. I hoped so, because for him to have distracted her meant something.

I got up from the table in my dining room and went to get the sausages out of the freezer for dinner, noticing there was a feeling of darkness in my energy. I couldn't tell what it was but needed to know, because I knew it had something to do with Pan; why else had it appeared in my space whilst thinking of her? Sitting back at the table, with a fresh cuppa tea, I googled Vancouver news. There was the usual celebrity bullshit and vacuous toxic who looks good or bad in whatever outfit and who's relationship was and was not going to last. Then as I clicked on business news I saw it; for the first time since knowing Pan I saw the face that haunted her deepest fears. "So that's what you look like, you arsehole," I said out loud, and he looked as smug as you like. He had one of those faces you just wanted to slap, and his energy was just pure evil, even through the photos he made your skin crawl.

As I read the headlines and the subtitles, I started to feel both relieved and angry. Relieved because he had been taken in for questioning and the 'investigation was ongoing' in one report, with 'mounting evidence' being reported by another; angry because his network of perversion was suspected to reach far and wide, with women, girls and young boys being the 'objects of desire' spanning across Canada. With his subsidiary companies in America, Europe and as far away as Australia, there was also suspicion as to what, if any, their involvement would be.

It looked like Pan had brought down a fucking massive house of cards and the more faces of those involved were shown in the press, the more of those who had been subjected to their evil came forward. Four decades, thousands of lives ruined directly as well as indirectly. I wanted to run up to her and hug her, but couldn't, so I picked up Shadow instead and started dancing in a kind of celebration that this had been uncovered and things were going to be put right. But the tears came, and they came hard and fast, for all those people around the world who had been violated, had their trust within themselves taken away. To know what had happened to my friend, to know that she had been part of this evil, and to know that she was the one who had taken the first step to unravel this network of evil. Like they said, there was a single thread that connected us all together and it only needed a single pull in the right direction for it to unravel in all directions.

Shadow looked at me, then jumped out of my arms and went to the doorway, turned around and beckoned me to the boot room. "Good idea. Where shall we go? In the car? Or to the moors?" As soon as I said the moors, his tail went crazy. "Okay, to the moors it is then." With that he ran to the boot room, jumped up and grabbed his lead. I loved this dog!

I knew I wouldn't get much work done for the rest of the afternoon after reading all that, so Shadow and I enjoyed the walk and then made our way to the school to pick up the boys on the bus. It would be nice not to have to think about driving, I'd rather be completely present to the boys. Seeing them both, I wrapped my arms around them tightly, thanking God for them and I breathed in their essence and prayed for them to always be protected.

"Are you okay Mama?" both of them asked when I hugged them.

"Yeah, I am good, just so grateful to have you both and know you are safe," I replied.

"Okay, what's happened?" asked my eldest.

"I just saw some really awful news stories that's all, ones that involved some really evil people who hurt women and children. Like I said, I am glad you are both safe and I have you both here with me to protect you and love you with all my heart and soul."

"I thought you didn't read the news?" questioned my youngest. "It's always full of bad news and fear, you said."

"I know Baaba, but sometimes when I get one of those feelings, and I do research, I discover things about the world that makes me sad, and makes me want to protect you from harm, without suffocating you, obviously. I know I have to share it with you in a way that makes you aware, when I have processed it myself, just know you always have a say in whatever happens to you in life, and always be confident to stand up to bullies, no matter how big they are or what they threaten you with."

"We know, and you're the best Mama," both boys said at once, as if rehearsed.

"I love you both so much."

"We know," answered my eldest.

"What's for dinner?" asked my youngest. "Can we have pancakes?"

I laughed, and smiles broke across their faces.

"We're having pancakes, aren't we? You were going to make them anyway, weren't you?" they chorused.

"I was, with some sausages, eggs and some spinach and garlic. What do you think?"

"Sounds great… but not too much spinach, you can have that," my youngest said giving my right arm a hug. "I love you Mama."

Emotions flooded my entire being and tears sprung up behind my eyes. "I love you too Baaba, both of you."

"We know. So are we going on a road trip tomorrow? It's Friday tomorrow," stated my eldest.

"I was thinking we could go west, to Wales. What do you think? Sound like a plan?"

"Yesss!!" they both said with excitement. "Hear that Shadow? We're going on a road trip tomorrow!"

Shadow wagged his tail and licked my eldest on the neck and chin, making him giggle. The best sound in the world, other than the boys breathing, was hearing them laugh. Man, I loved these boys, and God help anyone who hurt them.

With the radio on in the background, the three of us singing and dancing away to the music playing, we were just waiting for the sausages to finish baking.

"Are you on the radio again tomorrow Mama?" asked my youngest.

"I am, why?"

"Well, we only listen to the radio when you are going to be on the next day. So what are you talking about tomorrow?"

"Oh you know, everything and anything. Whatever comes up in the news, and about my new business," I answered.

"So you are not talking about your new book then?" asked my eldest.

"No, it doesn't seem right to talk about that one just yet, especially with everything that has happened with Baaba. I need to stop writing that one and focus on the business. I need to bring in some money, remember we will be moving soon, and I need to find us a new place to live," I answered, in hope that we would find a new place really soon.

We only had a month left in this place and although I would miss it, it was time to move on. I had chosen it for the four of us, and every time I looked into the dining room, I saw the boys sat playing mousetrap and being totally unaware that their world had just been turned upside down by their father. I needed to leave and create a new life for the three of us, a place we called home. I drifted off thinking of the kind of place I wanted for us all, not just the property, but the lifestyle, the local environment. It was time to let go of the past and focus on the future.

My mind wandered then to Pan, and I looked at the time. It was 5:55 pm exactly. I started smiling and chuckled to myself.

"What are you smiling at, Mama?" asked my youngest.

"Look at the time," I said, nodding towards the clock on the cooker.

"5:55 pm. Ah you and your angel numbers!" said my eldest laughing at me.

"What do these ones mean?" my youngest asked with real interest.

"Five five five? Means that the angels are sending me a message to let go of the past and all that is no longer serving me, and to trust that they will be replaced with better things moving forward."

"Ah cool! So we are moving in the next two weeks then?" said my youngest excitedly.

"Ahhhh you two!" my eldest laughed whilst putting his head in his hands. "You drive me crazy!"

At that moment the oven alarm went off and the sausages were ready. I took the food, my youngest took the plates and cutlery to the table, whilst my eldest took the jug of juice and the cups, and we sat down for our evening meal.

"Doesn't your friend, the email friend who goes diving, go on her holiday soon?" asked my eldest.

"She should have arrived at the hotel by now, yes. She's probably in the ocean now," I said smiling, that he had remembered.

"Cool. Does she do angel numbers too?" he asked.

"She calls it numerology, rather than angel numbers, and yes she does."

"Five five five would be good for her too then if she is in a competition in hot weather rather than cold weather, won't they?" chirped in my youngest.

"Yes it would Baaba, yes it would."

So I thought I would send you this email because no doubt you have seen the news unfolding back in Vancouver. Seems like I have opened a web of evil, hey? Well, it had to be done, right? I am glad I did it, and I am glad you asked me that question all those years ago. Thank you, really truly thank you my friend. I do love you, you know.

So no doubt you are wanting to know what I think of this place here in the middle of nowhere, with the stunning beaches, palm trees and temperatures like I have never known in my life. I got off the plane and thought my skin would melt from my bones, so you know what I did… I don't have to tell you, do I? Yep, straight into the ocean once I had checked in at the hotel, which is right on the fucking beach! Like seriously! I step out of my beautiful room right onto the beach! And there is this beautiful blue ocean, just calling my name. I fell asleep to the sound of the ocean last night and I actually thought to myself 'I could get used to this'. Honestly, it is just beautiful here, Mo. My white skin is not so white, pinker and in shock from all the Vitamin D it has absorbed since being here. I think it has had more Vitamin D in the last 48 hours than it has ever had! Still, good for the bones and muscles, which is pretty good for us divers, well necessary, I would say.

Speaking of divers, there are so many here. It's a little intense being around this many people, but it is nice to be around others who really get the thrill of being in the water for so long and going as deep as they can. There is a lot of talk about competitive apnea, and who can go deeper for longer, and go down as many times in one dive session, but all with humility. There are no egos here, which is a relief, just people who are really into just being in the water and pushing themselves to their limits, whilst also respecting the ocean. I did hear one guy talking about his last dive, which was a good reminder. He was saying that although he wanted to go just one more minute, he didn't want to be another body washed up on the beach, another casualty of the freediving community who hadn't paid attention to the 'matrix glitching'. I thought that was a good analogy and had to admire him for the depth of his respect for life and our sport. It's interesting hearing how people came to this sport, how some of them came from traditional spearfishing families, or had seen the fishermen whilst on holidays in the Philippines. Others started out scuba diving, or simply loved being under the water in the pool. Others like me study marine biology and ecosystems, and others just go a bit quiet and say they like the silence of being under water. I didn't know what to say when they asked me, so I said I was an accidental freediver, someone who found her passion through pain. A few nodded, one or two looked at me with intrigue, and all accepted it. And you know what Mo, I think I have found a new tribe here. We have only been together a few days, but sometimes you just know, isn't that what Nuliajuk said? Soul knows.

I was so happy to hear that she had found a special time and place to be, with kindred spirits of the ocean. She needed it, deserved it and I knew she would love every moment of being in warmer waters, with different marine ecosystems and mammals to study. I knew she would probably forgo her return flight back after the competition, choosing to stay on for longer 'to make the most of it whilst here' and I hope she would. A new environment away from everything and everyone who knew her, a fresh start would do her good, at least for now whilst the storm back in North America took over the news.

No reminders of the past at all.

Just Pan, her fins and the ocean.

GRATITUDE

When I first started writing my gratitude pages there were lots of people I would thank, but now as the number of books I write increases and the years are behind me, my inner circle is getting smaller.

That said this book would not be the work of art it is without the incredible talent of my dear friend and incredibly talented Jerry Lampson. How he comes up with the designs he does is beyond me. He even helped with the blurb this time! Go Jerry!

Linda, my right-hand woman, the one who sees my vision, calls me forward, makes sure the books get the love behind the scenes they need. I don't know what I would do without you my lovely. Here's to more papaya and avocado moments behind the scenes to keep us going!

To Adam, the man who holds space for the much-needed conversations this world needs to hear and who has blessed me with his audiophile talents with the podcasts for each book in *The Sacral Series*. Thank you for holding me during these conversations, steering the way and leading me through the process of podcasting.

To my mum and dad for our weekly calls, and my two incredible sons who all help me through the challenging moments of being on this unconventional journey of family life. Seeing your faces and hearing your voices keeps me going, keeps reminding me of the reasons I am here, of the people I am here to serve and why my work is so important.

Boys remember… you have a voice. Never be afraid to use it, ever. Stand in your power, your truth and always, always seek and speak your truth regardless of the outcome. I love you.

Dawn

ABOUT THE AUTHOR

With 20+ years of entrepreneurial experience, coaching and leading individuals and teams to outstanding results, Dawn Bates is one of the world's best kept secrets, and for good reason. Delivering impeccable service to her clients means she is selective in who she works with; her strong moral compass guides her to the projects she chooses to take on.

Dawn's repertoire of work is vast and her inquisitive mind astounding, bringing fresh insights and perspectives from 20 years of international travel and working in the UK, Europe, the Middle East and Australasia, with clients spanning five continents, multiple ethnicities, cultures and languages.

With a passion for leadership and cultural diversity, Dawn brings a wealth of knowledge and experience like no other. Her expertise lies in making you rethink your life and the world we live in, harnessing the deepest freedom of all: your own truth.

As well as being an international bestselling author, author strategist and ghostwriter, Dawn specialises in developing brand expansion, step change strategies and global visions, underpinned by her profound wisdom, truth slaying approach, high energy and trademark giggle.

She writes for various magazines, and when not sailing

around the world on yachts, she appears on various media channels highlighting and discussing important subjects in today's society.

She's an authority on leading others to create exceptional results by igniting the passions and fire deep within, shifting individuals and teams from disconnection, fear, feelings of imposter and self-doubt, to confidence, connection and courage to speak, live and work powerfully together with others.

To find out how you can work with Dawn, visit

www.dawnbates.com

If you have purchased a copy of this book, I would love for you to send me a selfie of you and my book.

Tag me on:

facebook.com/RealDawnBates

instagram.com/realdawnbates

twitter.com/realdawnbates

linkedin.com/in/dawnbates

…so I can thank you in person.

Ciao for now mi amore, and be blessed always x